George Augustin

Romances of New Orleans

George Augustin

Romances of New Orleans

ISBN/EAN: 9783337069094

Printed in Europe, USA, Canada, Australia, Japan

Cover: Foto ©Andreas Hilbeck / pixelio.de

More available books at **www.hansebooks.com**

N OR

BY GEO. AU

AUTHOR

Love and Death," "*Her Punish*

Mrs A. V

Though this transient world
As the countless ages ro.
What one seeks from man to hold
Will he struggle to control.
—*The Fleeting*

NEW ORLEANS:
L. GRAHAM & SON, 99-103 GRAVIER ST
1891.

PREFACE

The invariable rule of the general reader is to skip prefaces, but an author's immemorial habit being to write them, I feel myself called upon for an explanation. I will do so briefly and simply. I only wish to thank those who have kindly helped me in this undertaking. Being a New Orleans boy, substantial encouragement was generally tendered, assuring success.

A few of the poems and romances herein have already been published under my name in various periodicals. With but slight changes. I reproduce them as they originally appeared.

"Yetta. the Nun," has never been in print before. It is

> " A tale of sorrow treasured,
>   Too fondly to depart;
> Of wrong from Love the Flatterer,
>   And my own wayward heart,"

and has taken me four years to complete. It has been revised, altered and condensed more times than I can tell, and it is with mingled feelings of regret and reluctance that I now part with this favorite child of my fancy. Perchance some critical reader will begrudge me for having weaned it so soon?

G. A.

New Orleans, *March 16, 1891.*

CONTENTS.

YETTA, THE NUN,

A FORGOTTEN TRAGEDY OF OLD

NEW ORLEANS.

YETTA, THE NUN.

CHAPTER I.

Rise, O tide of my heart, to her beautiful eyes,
On the billows of Fate, like the sea to the skies.

About the year 1763, Dr. Carlos Alvez, a
graduate of the Madrid School of Medicine,
left his native country and settled in New
Orleans. He was young, intelligent and ambitious and soon controlled a numerous practice.
In a few years he amassed a snug fortune,
which he invested in town lots. Toward the
end of the last century he established a drug
store at the corner of Esplanade avenue and
Rampart street and did a thriving business.

Among the throngs which daily pass the locality, on their way to the business sections of
the city, probably not one ever heard of the
quaint little structure known as "Pharmacie
Alvez." It was destroyed by fire in 1836. A
one-story frame house, at present used as a

fruit stand and grocery combined, has oblit-
erated all signs of the old landmark.

Dr. Alvez prospered wonderfully. He gradually acquired possession of the land adjoining
his original purchase, until his estate included
all that tract now comprised within Esplanade
avenue, Burgundy, St. Anthony and St. Claude
streets.

In 1802 Dr. Alvez married Miss Pepita
Delric, daughter of a college-mate of his
father, who, like him, had made Louisiana
his home. A son (Louis) blessed this union.
From his infancy this young gentleman was
schooled to familiarize himself with the profession which had been followed by his paternal
ancestors from time immemorial. Dr. Alvez's
ambition was that his offspring should begin as
early as possible to assist him in ministering to
the ills of his numerous clientele and tradition
says he began "talking shop" to him on the
very day he had his first look at the world. In
after years, when young Louis had mastered
the alphabet and could read words of one
or two syllables, the first book of any conse-
quence he had to struggle with, was a medical
one. His father would take him on his knee

and expound things which made the toddler open his eyes to their widest capacity and cross-examine his instructor as only a child can. But the Doctor bore this catechism with fortitude and cheerfully explained everything.

Dr. Alvez's father-in-law had only two children— Pepita and Charles. The latter married a Creole girl a few years after the Doctor's inroad into the family and a daughter, Yetta, was born to him.

From the day Louis was allowed to take a peep at his new cousin, he evinced a strong interest in her. As time went by and the young lady began to understand what transpired about her, she reciprocated his affection and the two romped and played together, as happy as mortals could be. Very often, when evening came and their nurses would coax them to stop their gambols and retire peaceably to bed, they would cryingly protest against such an arbitrary procedure and force had to be employed to separate them.

At twelve years of age, Yetta was bundled off to a convent. Louis was two years her senior, and had attained an age at which most boys consider themselves full-grown men, but this

did not deter him from sobbing like a baby
when he received a scrawly, tear-bedewed note
from his little sweetheart a few days afterward,
in which she said she still thought as much of
him and had cried every night since their separa-
tion.

Yetta remained absent seven years. During
that period, Louis had news of her only
through her parents, as the nuns abhorred men,
and spirited away any communication addressed
to their wards. This is why Yetta never received the lurid answer Louis penned her.

A few now living may recall the peculiar,
semi-octagonal building which years ago stood
in the pentagon formed by Bourbon, Dauphine,
Union, Royal and Peace streets. This was
St. Veronica Convent. It was the first large
dwelling constructed in Louisiana, and was for
a long time an object of wondering admiration.
It was torn down and its site subdivided into
lots about forty years ago.

But the curiously inclined were not permitted
to inspect this quaint structure very minutely.
The nuns waged incessant war against in-
truders. The grounds were surrounded by
a high stone wall, topped with broken glass.

etc., and traps were hidden in the most out-of-the-way places within the shadow of the wall. There were large signs at each angle of the wall, on which was conspicuously painted:

NO BOYS OR MEN
ALLOWED ON THESE PREMISES.

Fearful stories were told of the fate of boys who had had the temerity to disregard this prohibition. There was a tradition, often whispered at the fireside with shuddering dread, that the nuns' favorite mode of punishment was to tie them by the feet to one end of a short rope, at whose other extremity a wildcat or panther was attached. The whole thing was then thrown over the limb of a tree reserved expressly for such exhibitions and the venturesome youth was never seen or heard of afterward. Other gruesome modes of punishment were vouched for, but this particular one had a more deterrent effect upon predatory urchins than any other.

This explains why, although living but a few squares from the convent, Louis never saw his child-love during the seven years she was away.

Years went by. Spurred by his ambitious
father Louis studied zealously, and at twenty-
one graduated with high honors. Of course
Dr. Alvez could not allow such an event to pass
quietly by. He gave a grand ball in his son's
honor, to which all the youth and beauty of
fashionable New Orleans were invited.

On the morning of the day selected for the
ball, Yetta returned from convent. Louis was
amazed at the change time had operated in her,
and wondered what mysterious agency could
have metamorphosed her into such a beautiful
woman. Up to that day he had never been
seriously in love. He had but a vague idea of
what this dangerous passion really was, and
little dreamed what momentous changes it could
work in the life of a man. He thought that
women were created simply to amuse us, and
the idea of manacling himself for life to one of
these effervescent beings never entered his mind.
As he contemplated Yetta on the night of the
ball, all his pet theories were forgotten. He
pictured to himself what bliss it would be to
pass one's entire life near her, a slave to her
every wish. Memories of the past, dormant for
years, whirled through his mind. He imagined

himself walking hand in hand with his child
love through his father's park, happy, innocent,
thinking only of frolicking about. Could her
heart still be beating for him, or had the advent
of womanhood banished the past from her mind?
He felt bewildered, fascinated, and would have
parted with the dearest treasures of earth to be
left alone with her for a single moment, that he
might implore her to unbind the fetters she had
gyved around his heart years ago.

Having been immured for seven dreary years
in an institution where even to mention a mas-
culine name evoked a frowning rebuke, Yetta
naturally had an unconquerable horror of the
dance. It was only after much coaxing that she
consented to remain in the parlor; and being a
woman of tact and education, she took pains to
make herself agreeable.

Louis spent much of his time beside his
cousin. Not to appear too boorish, he was compelled to be amiable with all; but whenever he
could escape, he would seek Yetta.

"Your guests will think you very uncivil,"
said the latter, as Louis approached her and
asked the privilege of a promenade. "You are
too often near me."

2

"I have the reputation of being a desperate flirt," Louis observed; "this will shield me from censure."

Yetta laughed softly and accepted his proffered arm.

They were now in the garden. It was the first time the cousins had a chance to be alone, and Louis resolved to know his fate. He began by talking of the past, and asked Yetta if she recalled the delightful times they had together. To his surprise she seemed displeased, and petulantly said:

"Let us leave our childhood days alone, I entreat you. I have been so long away from the world that I want to hear of *present* happenings."

Louis tried to conquer this whim, but seeing he only succeeded in getting Yetta angry, concluded he would have plenty of time to make her talk the ensuing days and turned the conversation into other channels.

The rest of the evening seemed like a dream to the young doctor. He felt he had at last met his Waterloo; that women were not created simply to amuse us, but to sway our souls with their gentleness and fascinating sweetness.

CHAPTER II.

" I'll obey you, though 't is plain
You are jesting with my pain."

For a week after Yetta's arrival, Louis saw
her only at meals, as his father kept him clos-
eted all day in his laboratory, instructing him
how to compound innumerable chemical com-
positions and making him delve into almost in-
terminable volumes to more fully illustrate his
teachings.

When the young man was at last liberated,
he felt overjoyed and roamed all about the
house in search of his ideal. He thought how
glad she would be to have a few hours of undisturbed conversation with her childhood companion ; how volubly they would speak of the
delightful events of the past. He attributed her
previous restraint to her sudden transition from
the dismal quietness of convent life to the dizzy
turmoil of the social world, and wondered what
queer notions went tumbling about her puzzled
little head. She would see her child-lover
once more, would confide to him as of old and
would find his heart yearning to call back the
feeling which had been dormant so long.

What dreams—but his reverie was brought to an
end by his coming suddenly upon Yetta, who
stood in a doorway overlooking the garden,
gazing dreamily about. This incident, coupled
with his romantic train of thoughts, served to
completely demoralize him. The great love
he felt for his cousin overmastered all thoughts
of further restraint and he rushed forward,
caught her in his arms and showered kiss after
kiss upon her roseal, half-parted lips.

"Oh Louis, how you frightened me!" exclaim-
ed the girl, freeing herself from his grasp.
"Were I your father," she angrily resumed,
"I would keep you locked up all the time.
You are positively dangerous."

"What a fine young lady you are," Louis
admiringly said, not heeding her anger. "It
seems to me as if it were but yesterday that we
romped together. What a rousing girl you
are!"

He advanced with the intention of repeating
the osculatory performance.

"I wish you would stop those ungentlemanly
manners," Yetta curtly said, pushing him away.
"I think over-study has taken away the little
intelligence you once possessed."

Louis had expected a more amiable reception.

"Such a compliment should be punished with a kiss," he replied, affecting gayety.

"Love may cherish such punishments," was the chilling reply; "indifference detests them."

Louis made no reply, but gazed amusedly at the angry girl, curious to discover what could be her motive in being so curt. He observed that her lips trembled like those of a frightened child, and plainly saw she was far from meaning what she said. He felt an irresistible yearning to take her again in his arms and kiss those pouting lips until they smiled for him; but the harsh manner in which she had spoken had wounded his pride, and he did not care to be too effusive without first teasing her a little. Smiling derisively, he said:

"Your conduct is not very laudable, Yetta."

"I am aware of it," was the quick retort.

"Then why do you act that way?"

"Because I do not care to remodel my character to suit your fancy."

Louis bit his lip and changed his tone to one of conciliation.

"Come," he said, "look gay and do not be

so mean. Suppose we stroll about the gardens?
It is such a fine evening for walking."

"I thank you ever so much, but I am tired,"
was the answer.

"Tired?" Louis testily exclaimed. "That
word never escaped your lips years ago—"

Yetta impatiently interrupted him.

"I wish you would cease importuning me
about my baby days," she said. "I told you it
displeased me."

Louis gazed sadly at her.

"Do I annoy you?" he asked.

"When you speak of our childhood—yes."

"You really do not care to listen to me?"

"I have proved it often enough."

"It would then cause you unutterable joy if I
left you alone?"

"I assure you it would."

"Very well, marble-hearted, convent-bred
girl, I will pester you no more."

He abruptly left the room. Yetta looked on
with unmoved features, but a tear coursed down
her cheek as her lover disappeared from sight.

One morning, Louis rose earlier than usual
and wandered about the garden, pondering over
the singularity of Yetta's conduct. Whenever

Dr. Alvez or any member of the family were present, she was amiable, even affectionate with him, but she would immediately assume an attitude of exasperating coldness should she find herself alone with him and finally leave the room on some trifling pretext.

"That girl is a born coquette," mused Louis, walking aimlessly about. "I never had a flattering opinion of convents,—Hello!"

He had come around a sharp turn of the path and found himself face to face with Yetta, who was reclining in an easy chair, apparently deeply interested in an illustrated magazine. She seemed not to have noticed the intruder.

"Let me try a reconciliation," thought Louis. "Perhaps she is in good humor this morning."

He advanced toward her and pleasantly said:

"Up already, cousin? This is quite an unexpected pleasure."

Yetta kept on reading with unaltered persistency.

Louis gulped down an angry remark and gallantly resumed:

"A Madonna would envy your grace, Yetta.

You are as appetizing as a rose bud this morning."

He made a feint of kissing her, She edged
away a little and fixed her dark eyes upon him.

" I detest time-worn compliments," she said.

" I will cheerfully coin new ones to please
you," answered Louis.

Again those dark eyes were raised to his face
in frowning rebuke.

" I wish you would talk and act sensibly once
in your life," said their owner, coldly. " I am
tired to hear everybody say we are going to
marry, and I want to come to some definite
understanding with you: Do you really love
me?"

The suddenness of the question took Louis
by surprise.

" It would be folly to deny it," he wonderingly replied.

" I felt sure of it," Yetta resumed, " but I
wanted to hear you say so. Perhaps I also love
you, but I can not confess it. You do not understand my nature, Louis. You think me
haughty and cruel; could you read my thoughts
you would unhesitatingly pity me. I know I
I make you suffer, but you are not the only

one who feels miserable. Could you be near when I am alone in my room and see the tears that veil my eyes when I ponder over my happy, innocent childhood; could you listen to the beating of my aching heart, you would kneel before me and implore my pardon for every unkind word you spoke to me."

"Sweet love," said Louis, fondly, "If you only knew how dear you were to me."

He made an effort to take her in his arms, but the girl pushed him away, saying:

"No, Louis, I can never be yours. My heart may be longing to remain amid associations of a life which I can never revive, but I must steel it against such thoughts. I must return to convent next week. If you have any compassionate feeling for me, do not make the parting harder. Even if I am rude with you, be kind to me, forgive me!"

She glanced imploringly at him. He started, for he saw in that look the unconscious avowal of a deep, passionate love, whose fervency only death could obliterate. He felt like folding her to his bosom; but she had so often repulsed him, he remained impassive.

"I admire your frankness, Yetta," he said,

quietly. "I hardly comprehend your motive, but I respect it. Were you my wife, my pathway through life would be strewn with thornless roses; but you deny me that happiness and I will do as you wish. Give me your hand. If we can not be lovers, we can at least part as friends."

He extended his hand, but Yetta eluded it.

"I care no more for your friendship than I do for your love," was the haughty remark. "I thought you loved me truly and felt sorry for you, knowing I could never be your wife. The nuns rightly told me that all men were fickle and false-hearted, and it was foolish of me to believe you sincere for a single moment. If you really cared for me, you would not have proved so faint-hearted; you would have begged me to marry you with all the ardor which true love inculcates. Instead of giving me up so easily, you would now be on your knees before me."

Louis looked coldly at her.

"I have never knelt before a woman," he said; "I never will."

He walked rapidly away to conceal his agitation. When he had got around the turn in the path, he stopped, softly retraced his steps and peeped at the scene he had just left. Yetta's head was laid on her arm and he could see by her trembling form that she was sobbing. A satisfied smile displaced the frown which had darkened his features and he walked away with a happier heart. He was now certain of her love.

A few hours later a servant brought the young doctor the appended note:

"DEAR LOUIS—I hope you are not angry because I treated you so unkindly this morning. I felt nervous and did not mean half the things I said. I am going to make a pilgrimage to the Lover's Oak just now; meet me there as soon as you can escape from that nasty old laboratory and we can talk about anything you like.
"YETTA."

Louis tore the note into minute pieces.

"I will do no such thing," he said. "If she thinks she can make a jumping-jack out of me, she is mistaken. Hang those convent girls, anyhow. I wonder if they are all as chameleon-like as Yetta?"

He went to his desk and began to attend to routine business. By some inexplicable phenomenon, the miscellaneous rows of jars and bottles about him gradually vanished and there arose in their stead a stately oak, near which bubbled a little fountain. He looked on more intently. A human form slowly outlined itself, finally disclosing a saddened, expectant face, whose dark eyes were wistfully turned toward him. He rubbed his eyes and looked again— but only saw medical paraphernalia.

"If that girl does not drive me crazy with her sorcery," he muttered, "I am endowed with phenomenal mental calibre."

He arose with a sigh and went toward the designated place.

CHAPTER III.

" See here: I shut tight my weary eyes,
    As thousands of times I've done in play.
When I unclose them in soft surprise,
    Ring out a laugh in your own old way ! "

Louis entered the garden with wildly beating heart, and hastened his steps when he neared the Lover's Oak—so called because it had been the trysting-place of amorous couples from time immemorial. As he drew near, however, the spirit of aggressiveness which had ruled since the lovers had been thrown together, prompted him to open hostilities, and he walked toward Yetta with the avowed intention of getting her angry. Seeing she had not noticed his coming, he hid behind a tree and indulged in the intellectual pastime of watching her every movement. She was knitting, and the sight seemed to Louis the prettiest he had ever witnessed.

For a few moments Yetta went on with her work in silence; then, looking up, quietly said:

"It seems to me it is quite warm to play hide-and-seek, doctor. Come and sit near me."

How gently she spoke! Louis stared speechlessly at her, wondering if he was not the victim of a delicious vision.

"I see that you are revengeful, continued Yetta, in the same tone. "Do not be that way. See, I have made a nice, cosy place for you."

And she pushed aside her work.

"I am sure you must think me very stupid," said Louis, taking the proffered seat.

"Not at all. You are a little eccentric, that is all. But you are a doctor and this foible is pardonable. By the by, we have spent so much time wrangling about one thing and another, that you did not once speak to me

about your future plans or your profession.   I
think it is such a noble one.   Confide all your
secrets to me, Louis."

She leaned her head upon her hand and
looked encouragingly at him.   Louis' first
thought was that she was making fun of him,
and he opened his mouth to say something unkind ; but those clear eyes looking straight into
his own disarmed him, and the harsh words
remained unuttered.

"Do you really care to listen to me?" he
asked, for want of something else to say.

" If I was not interested in your welfare,
I would not have called you here," was the re-
proving answer.

Louis hesitatingly pressed her hand.   She
made no resistance.   He then tried to speak,
but the phrases he wished to utter went whirling
about his mind in such wild disorder, that he
merely stared at the girl and kept on pressing
her hand.   Yetta's face became a deep pink all
over, the color going and coming like the soft-
ening glow of a dying ember.

" Why are you holding my hand so tightly
and looking at me in such a funny way?" she
queried, poutingly.

"I—er—that is—er—I was trying to—er—mesmerize you," stammered the doctor, hazarding any reply.

Yetta looked at him in sincere wonder.

"I don't understand, Louis. Please explain."

Louis was but slightly familiar with this mysterious science; nevertheless, he began a graphic portraiture of its effects on certain persons, the utopian experiments he had witnessed, etc., concluding by getting things so hopelessly confused, that Yetta smilingly interrupted:

"I can not understand your meaning, but it is not your fault if I am dull of comprehension. From the faint knowledge I glean from your explanation, I think it must be so nice to be mesmerized. Could you not try again? I promise not to disturb you."

The unwilling champion of Mesmer winced a little, but it was too late to retreat.

"You must then remain perfectly still and look me straight in the eyes," he gravely remarked.

Yetta did so.

Louis arose, made a few passes, and said:

"Don't you feel a little drowsy?"

"Never was so wide awake in my life."

"This is the precursor of the magnetic cur

rent," observed the experimenter, feeling it mandatory to say something.

He next indulged in a nondescript pantomime.

"Are you asleep now?" he asked, faintly.

"Not a bit," was the discouraging reply.

Again Louis made spasmodic passes, but Yetta's eyes shone with tantalizing clearness.

"It is not right to act that way," complained the doctor. "You *must* go to sleep."

"But I don't feel any magnetic current. You know you said this was the principal thing in mesmerism."

"That's nothing; shut tight your eyes and you will feel it quick enough."

She languidly closed her eyes. Louis waited a few moments and said :

"Are you asleep now?"

"Yes."

"Fast asleep?"

"Nothing but your domineering mind can awake me."

The situation was getting embarrassing. Louis knew she was dissembling.

"I experience a fond longing to pry into the secrets of your heart," he said, in deep, thrilling tones.

" My heart is no longer in my power," came the response, in a voice so low that the hypnotizer had to bend very near to distinguish the sounds.

" What audacious mortal has dominion over it?" he said, breathlessly.

" The one whose subtle influence has over-mastered my volition."

"And the owner of the heart, has she —"

" I divine your thoughts ere you can utter them. No, she has no desire to recall it."

Her answers flashed like lightning!

"Never mind," thought Louis, " I'll give you tit for tat."

He noiselessly slipped away and walked behind Yetta, intending to take her by surprise and kiss her upturned lips. He slowly stooped over her. Nearer and nearer were her lips; wilder and wilder beat his heart. Only one second and he would have tasted the prohibited ambrosia—but the queenly head was swiftly averted, and he only kissed a fluttering curl.

Louis was naturally indignant.

"I thought you were asleep," he said, frowning.

" I am. See, my eyes are closed."

"How then could you have seen me stooping down?"

"I did not see you. I read what was going on in your mind."

"How can you read what was going on in my mind, when it is *I* who mesmerized you? You are a little imposter, Yetta."

"You have mastery over me in all matters which do not appertain to loving demonstrations—but no further. The moment you feel the least desire to take familiarities with me, your dominion ceases. A *touch* suffices to transfer your will power to me."

"The pupil seems to know more than its instructor," mused Louis. "Let me formulate a poser. Ah, I have it!"

He again faced her and gravely observed:

"By the mastery my will exercises over thine, O! dormant girl, I command thee to warble a fervid love sonnet—a tune which no mortal ears have yet heard and which mortal lips have yet to utter. Selah! I have spoken."

A slight tremor passed over the girl and her face was very pale as she replied:

"Director of my subservient mind, must I

chant of the blissful past, the troublous present or the veiled future?"

"Thy song must allude to those three phases of life," was the triumphant response.

Yetta slightly raised her head and sang the following strain, in a voice scarcely audible at first, but which gradually became louder and clearer as she proceeded:

PARTED.

We must part!
   Ah, my tones quaver
 And my blanched cheeks paler seem;
Can it be that I shall never
 See thine eyes with love-looks beam?
Thou art pensive 'cause my cold hand
 Trembles as it fondles thine,
Telling of wounds which can ne'er mend—
 Wounds enshrined by arts of thine.

Courage!
   See, my lips are smiling
 And my voice hath ceased to quaver;
Press my hand just once, my darling,
 Ere we drift apart forever.
Though from thy side I now hasten,
 Still thy dear face e'er will haunt me—
Love, I see thy fond eyes glisten;
 Is it—is it— No, I must flee!

Farewell!
           As the waning starbeams
    Linger in the morning sky;
As the Orient gleams with sunbeams
    And the dawn of day is nigh—
Still, my lover, I'll be thinking
    Of a face which makes mine glow,
And my white lips will be pleading:
    "Darling, *'t is not* time to go!"

As the final notes of the song floated away, gradually blending with the trillings of the birds, Louis caught Yetta in his arms and passionately embraced her. She gave a startled cry and rushed away from him.

CHAPTER IV.

"There is no death! The stars go down
  To rise upon some fairer shore;
And, bright in Heaven's jeweled crown,
  They shine forevermore."

Louis pressed his hands to his forehead and thought over the occurrences of the past weeks, feeling certain he would become mad if Yetta kept on tantalizing him much longer. Hearing a slight noise, he turned around,— and there stood Yetta, calmly looking at him!

" For God's sake, stop tormenting me!" he cried, putting forth his hands as if to push her away. " I have no strength left to defend myself."

" I do not come to torment you," sadly replied Yetta, resuming her seat. " If any one has cause to make reproaches, I should do so. I was playing with you, and you should not have taken advantage of my defenceless condition. You have wronged me deeply, Louis, for I now feel I can never conquer the sentiment I have for you."

She buried her face between her hands and sobbed. Louis drew her gently to him and soothingly caressed her. She presently became calmer and said, suddenly :

" Is it true that all men are fickle-hearted and false? "

" With a single exception, yes."

" That exception is yourself?"

" Of course."

" You then never loved before?"

" No."

" Never even had a sweetheart! "

" You are a walking catechism, Yetta."

" You do not answer my question."

" Yes, I did have some. But this does not signify that I loved. All young men are— "

"Never mind other men. I want to know how many sweethearts you have had thus far."

" That's a funny question. I would answer with pleasure, but I lost the set of books in which I kept their names."

He smiled, but Yetta looked compassionately at him.

" You are very young to speak so banteringly about such a grave subject," said she. " Do you mean to tell me that you have loved, adored and forgotten—all within the brief transition from adolescence to manhood?"

"Such is the astounding truth."

Again Yetta looked pityingly at him.

"You are indeed worthy of commiseration," she observed, shaking her head. "I wonder if God will forgive you when the Day of Judgment arrives."

"I do not believe in such things," said Louis.

"Do you mean to say you do not think the soul is immortal?"

"I have faith in the soul's immortality, but not in a general day of judgment."

"I fail to understand your meaning, Louis."

"I will make it clearer: You believe in the

revival from the dead, and feel certain the day will come when an angel will descend from Heaven and warn mankind of its approaching doom. The tombs throughout the world will then crumble into dust, and their erst soulless tenants will be vivified and will throng the earth once more. This looks very pretty as an allegorical dissertation, but can never happen in reality. When a human being dies his soul returns to its Maker, who allots it to a place suited to its deportment while roaming the earth. In the meantime the lifeless clay has been entombed, and soon crumbles into dust. Thus nothing is left of the original shape. Centuries drag by. This residue of a once animated creation is gradually absorbed by the atmosphere, vanishing forever as time rolls on. Now, if there is any such thing as a general Day of Judgment, how can all the particles originally composing the body be reassembled into a compact mass? Can the elements restore the dust they have wafted throughout the Universe, and which has been mingling with the exudations from millions upon millions of soulless bodies for ages past? It is undeniably impossible."

Yetta seemed bewildered.

" And the soul, Louis," said she, "is its mission ended when it leaves the body?"

" No, it is immortal. If it is a crime-haunted soul, it is whirled into the deepest abyss of the infernal regions, where it squirms in eternal agony. If, on the contrary, its career has been pure, it is sent into other worlds, where it enters the body of a new-born babe and shields its after life from harm."

" The soul is then simply one's guardian angel?"

" You may call it thus."

Yetta remained thoughtful for a few moments.

" You speak of other worlds, Louis," she soon resumed. wonderingly; "what do you mean by this?"

" Every star in the firmament is more or less populated."

The girl fixed her troubled gaze upon her cousin.

" The nuns never told me all this," said she, simply. " I was made to believe that there was nothing but gaping nothingness beyond the clouds. Is there no limit to the universe, Louis."

"Space is unfettered by measurement. Beyond this world are others. Above, around— everywhere you may look, a star will always greet your vision. This star is a living world, peopled with beings who, as they glance in our direction, perhaps wonder what is that insignificant speck in the heavens, billions of miles from them."

"How strange all this is," vaguely observed Yetta. "I never would have dreamed that such wonderful things existed. What will become of all these planets, Louis, when the end of the world comes? Will they all unite in a solid mass, or—or—"

She stopped short and looked helplessly at the doctor, who smiled at her bewilderment.

"I—I can not conjecture," she said. "The subject is too deep for me."

"The world will never come to an end," Louis quietly said. "The earth might be shattered, stars may forsake their courses and crash against each other through space, but there will always be millions left—thousands of new ones created out of their chaos."

"Matter is then imperishable?"

"The reconstruction of the universe goes on

everlastingly. Watch the sky attentively for a
few weeks and you will notice its changeability.
All around us old worlds are dying out and new
ones springing from their ruins. This is evi-
denced by the fact that stars which were plainly
visible to the naked eye years ago suddenly disappear and are never seen again. The fixed
stars that you admire so much on a radiant
night may have been annihilated centuries ago:
the light which reaches your vision is simply its beam, which has perhaps been travel-
ing through space since its source was shattered
cycles ago. This explains why you sometimes
see a star suddenly flare with intensity, then as
swiftly die out. It is the tale of a catastrophe
which happened long years ago, ere your great-
great-grandparents were born."

"How frightful!" exclaimed Yetta, pressing
closer to the speaker. "It makes me shiver to
think of all this. Is it really true that all things
will never come to an end?"

"The machinery of the universe will never
stop. Matter is indestructible; the soul immortal. When your heart's pulsations are stilled
and your lips closed in icy immutability, your
soul soars through space, speeding on, on, on,

until it reaches the throne of the Ever Living, the God who moulded it. It may then be sent to animate a human frame millions—aye, billions—of leagues away, but the time comes when it also abandons this clayey tenement and seeks another habitation. Thus it wanders with ceaseless toil until centuries and centuries pass by and the universe is studded anew with worlds."

Yetta pressed her hands to her temples.

"I—I can not countenance it," she faltered. "All this is beyond my comprehension and makes my thoughts whirl as leaves in the grasp of a hurricane."

She cast down her eyes and was soon lost in meditation.

CHAPTER V.

"Now back to the world and let Fate do her worst
On the heart that for thee such devotion hath nursed."

Louis had reached the conclusion that Yetta had this time permanently strayed into dreamland, when she suddenly remarked:

"I have seriously considered the matter and

I think it is best we should never marry. As I have not yet taken the veil, the Church would release me from my hasty vow, but I am afraid to be free. I can never have unlimited confidence in you. You are too learned in worldly ways. You are an irredeemable inconstant and can never make me happy.''

'' You are evidently losing your temper, my dear,'' said Louis, amusedly. '' Come, let us kiss and make up. You know I adore you.''

He put his arm around her waist, but she angrily pushed it away.

''Do not touch me!'' she exclaimed, scornfully. '' This self-same expression you have repeated to as many girls as were foolish enough to listen to you, and the caresses you wish to give me have•been lavished upon women whose features you do not even remember. How can I help doubting your sincerity? I have bared my heart to you, telling you all my sorrows, yet you look on with pitiless indifference, turning into ridicule everything I say.''

Louis hesitatingly approached her. She did not repel him, but fixed her troublous eyes reproachfully upon his face.

'' God knows I do not act thus to pain you,''

he kindly said. "You are the most volcanic, most romantic girl I ever met, and I am sure you do not mean half the things you say. The nuns have taught you from girlhood to think that way and you can not help it. When you have seen a little of the world, you will laugh at those fantastic ideas, which one only meets in sensational novels."

Yetta looked thoughtfully at the speaker, but said nothing. Encouraged, he resumed:

"Let us put a stop to this nonsense, Yetta. I love you sincerely, and life without you would be shorn of all that is sublime in the world."

Yetta thrust her hand in her bosom and drew forth a small crucifix.

"Kiss this holy cross and swear by the Divinity we both adore that you are serious," she said.

Louis looked at the earnest girl in speechless wonder.

"Do you refuse?" she asked, tremulously.

The young doctor pressed the sacred metal to his lips.

"I swear I love you truly," he said, his voice trembling with suppressed emotion.

"What further proof do you want? Speak and you will be obeyed."

Yetta replaced the crucifix in her bosom and said:

"I am satisfied, Louis. You may be false-hearted, but I believe you are honorable and would not perjure yourself to please a woman. I love you, but how can I know my passion is lasting? You are the first man who has ever kissed me, the only one who has talked so strangely sweet to me, and I can not help feeling for you a fascination which I can not define. Suppose I become your bride and then meet the one I am destined to love unreservedly, what will become of me? I would break your heart and lose my soul forever." She stopped a moment, then resumed: "Let us estrange ourselves for a year. During that time I will go into society, encourage admirers and flirt with whomsoever I fancy. If I love you truly, my heart will remain unchanged; if I am simply infatuated, you will be saved the humiliation of marrying a woman who cared but lightly for you."

Louis gazed amazedly at his cousin. Of all her queer notions, this certainly was the most

extraordinary. Surely, true love could never
harbor in such a hardened heart. He had
blindly trusted her, feeling certain she cared for
him, and the idea that she was perhaps toying
with him made the blood surge through his
veins like molten lava. The madcap blood of
his Spanish ancestors made the sting of defeat
still more penetrating. He controlled himself,
however, and said, in tones he vainly strove to
render dispassionate:

"You had better become a nun, Yetta. It
would be decidedly unwise for you to marry;
you might tire of your husband ere the honey-
moon is over and cry for your cherished convent."

He approached nearer to her and continued,
getting angrier at every sentence:

"Return to your nunnery, misguided girl,
and remain there until eternity. Seek salvation
in the arms of those pale-faced nuns. Let
them pray night and day to remove the stain my
caresses have engrafted on your soul. In after
years, when the voice which now blanches your
cheeks and kindles your eyes with sudden flame
is forever hushed, you will perhaps give a sorrowful thought to the memory of one whose re-

jected love your whole soul yearns to recall.
When you—"

But the sentence remained unfinished. Her
eyes flashing with the fire of wounded pride,
Yetta angrily pressed her hand to his mouth,
checking his mad-brain speech. She then
placed a trembling hand on his arm and said:

"I will make you regret those words, impetuous boy! I will not return to convent, but will
remain to wring your heart with despair and
make you idolize me still more fondly than you
now do. I swear by the memory of my saintly
ancestors that I love you; but you might implore me to marry you a thousand times more
madly than you have thus far done—I will never
be yours!"

She attempted to rise, but Louis grasped her
arm and compelled her to sit beside him again.

"You swear you will never marry," he exclaimed in faltering tones. "This is idle talk,
imperious girl! You love me, distractedly, and
it lies within my power to make you sway to my
will. You *will* be my wife, I tell you! I will
fan your passion into such soul-consuming
fierceness that you will weepingly seek me and
implore me on bended knees to assuage your
anguish!"

Yetta looked defiantly at him. Pushing him away from her, she quietly arose and walked off. Involuntarily, Louis stretched forth his arms, hoping she would turn back, but she kept firmly on and soon vanished through the sombre oaks.

CHAPTER VI.

Love, when true, can never die;
Sweethearts part, but still they sigh.

From the time of their stormy interview under the Lovers' Oak, the cousins never met without exchanging unkind words. Everywhere they found themselves face to face, they would contradict each other on the simplest subjects, smiling pleasantly all the while, but choosing expressions they knew would lacerate the heart at which it was aimed.

Louis soon felt he was growing into a state of alarming professional uselessness. He lost all interest in medical subjects, his thoughts wandering to Yetta or some particular act of annoyance he could do her, whenever he began any rational work. He finally resolved to bring

4

matters to a crisis. He had tried all he could
to make her consent to become his bride and
he would now attempt a last ruse—make love to
another girl. He knew what a potent factor
jealousy was in love. He had proofs that
it was a passion which corroded the pur-
est hearts and burned a pathway to the
deepest recesses of the soul. He no more
doubted that Yetta loved him. Often he felt
tempted to kneel before her and implore
her to ease his anguish; but the demon of pride
would stalk before him and chill any conciliatory
demonstrations.

Louis soon had an opportunity to begin
carrying his idea into execution. Dr. Alvez's
business increasing, he procured the services
of an eminent American chemist, Mr. Carleton
Hevlin, who was given a suite of rooms in the
Doctor's residence.

Mr. Hevlin was a widower. He had only
one child, Lulie, a sweet, blue-eyed lassie of
seventeen.

Of course it seemed perfectly natural that
Louis should be amiable with Lulie. Being his
guest, it was his duty to see that she was well
cared for and felt no restraint in her new home.

How well he discharged his task, will be seen later on.

A strong friendship had sprung between Lulie and Yetta. This at first annoyed Louis and made him doubt the feasibility of his plan, but he rightly concluded that the proud girl kept her secret locked in her breast and Lulie suspected nothing.

Child that he was to thus trifle with love. His insane wish to render Yetta jealous made him blind to everything. He never gave consideration to the fact that Lulie was young and inexperienced and little suspected what ravages he was working in her trusting heart. He merely noticed Yetta's restless look whenever he went out alone with his new love, and smiled contentedly.

One evening Louis entered the parlor and found only Yetta present.

"Where's Lulie?" he queried, with feigned annoyance.

"She is in the garden," replied Yetta, indifferently "I can spare your company."

Louis thoughtfully contemplated his cousin.

"Suppose I find this spot more attractive?" he observed, seating himself near by.

"I would leave you in undisputed possession of it," retorted Yetta, walking out of the
room.

"She is getting paler day by day," mused
Louis, a remorseful sensation in his breast.
"But she looks so beautiful when her eyes
flash in anger—when her bosom heaves with
suppressed emotions and her fingers tremble to
clutch and hurt me—that it would be a pity to
give up Lulie. You make me suffer, overproud
girl, but two can play at that game."

He repressed a sigh and went in search of
Lulie. As he neared the end of the path leading to the summer–house, he perceived her
seated at a window, busily knitting. She
feigned not to have noticed his coming, but her
nervousness betrayed her.

Louis stepped to the window and stood looking at her.

"Cruel girl!" he reproachfully said, pinch-
ing her tempting pink ear.

She gave a cry of joyful surprise.

"Is that you, Louis?" she exclaimed. "You
came in so noiselessly, I did not hear you."

"You are a little story-teller," was the laughing rejoinder. "You *did* see me coming, and I defy you to look into my face and deny it. Bring that dear head closer that I may kiss those cherub lips."

"No you won't," answered Lulie, drawing back a little; "I don't think it's nice manners."

Louis moodily walked up the steps and sat down in a remote corner.

"Are you angry?" said Lulie, seating herself near him; "I'm sure I said nothing to hurt your feelings."

"You refused to kiss me," muttered Louis, sadly.

Lulie laughed merrily.

"Is that all?" she said; "I do not deny it."

"And I, who thought myself so welcome when I was beside you," sighed the hypocrite.

Lulie fixed her gaze on the ground.

"I *can not* kiss you," she said, lowly.

Louis looked apprehensively at her. Could Yetta have been opening her eyes to the true state of things?

"Why this sudden coolness, Lulie?" he said, uneasily. "See how close my lips are: you

have merely to turn your head a little to touch
them with yours."

"It would not be right for me to do so," was
the gentle response. "Last night I was count-
ing the kisses you had stolen from me, and I
did not have enough fingers to check them all.
So I resolved to put a stop to these familiarities. You might see nothing wrong now, but
later on you will say: 'That girl allowed me
to kiss her without being engaged to me; of
course I can't marry her.' That's the way
men are."

She gave a decided toss of her golden
curls. Louis felt relieved and smiled at her
oddity.

"You are a grand rascal," he said. "Suppose I was your affianced, would you kiss me?',

"I presume so. That is what people get
engaged for."

"I do not know how to begin," was the
mournful plaint.

"What an absent-minded boy you are! Why,
you have asked me to marry you at least a
dozen times in your poems."

"Poetry and reality are different things."

"Well, I guess I'll have to teach you."

She put aside her work. Louis curiously watched her, but was not allowed a long time for observation. Seating herself with an air of unruffled dignity, the self-appointed preceptor began :

"You must first clasp my hand."

Louis did so.

"Now, look as if you expected the earth was going to swallow you up."

An agonized expression overspread his countenance.

"You must now go on your knees before me —how your hand trembles! It is not yet time to tremble; this comes only *after* kneeling."

Louis hesitated. The words he had repeated to Yetta, "*I have never knelt before a woman; I never will*," rang in his ears.

"How pale you are, Louis," resumed Lulie. "Kneel before your queen; I promise she will not be tyrannical."

He obeyed. The vibrations of his heart were painfully irregular; but he looked up into Lulie's smiling face and the pain was somewhat eased.

"Now," resumed the gentle autocrat, "prepare for the ordeal. Look as miserable as you

can and say in trembling tones: ' Miss Hevlin,
ever since my gaze rested on your seraphic
features I have worshiped you night and day.
Consent, O! enchanting miss, to become my
bride, or my existence will be an eternity of
despair.' "

Louis repeated the sentence word for word.

" Your sentiments find an echoing thrill in
my heart, imploring youth," resumed Lulie,
sweetly bending over her lover. "Assume your
customary attitude and be welcome to all the
privileges of an affianced."

Before Louis had time to arise, she playfully
passed her arm around his neck and pressed her
lips to his. It was a pure, girlish embrace,
free from voluptuousness—just the sort of caress one would expect from a mirthful child.
This innocent' demonstration of love caused an
enthralling sensation to possess the unhappy
young doctor. For the first time since parting
from Yetta he really felt happy. He reasoned
that the love of this dear girl would be a greater
boon to him than the passion of a convent-bred
creature, whose untenable way of thinking
would always prompt her to render his life miserable.

He sat beside Lulie with the old sensation of tranquillity in his breast, and fondly said:

"You do not know, my darling, how happy I am, now that I feel assured you really care for me. Come, let us walk around the garden. The birds will watch us with envious eyes and the heavens will bend over us and bless our happiness. Come, sweetness."

He arose and extended his hand. Lulie gleefully grasped it and they ran down the steps like madcap children. A pet rabbit of Lulie's, which happened to be peacefully dozing in a corner, looked up in affright at the lovers' sudden exit and bolted away as fast as its little legs could carry it. Lulie chased it, but it soon outstripped her and disappeared in the shrubbery. Ere Louis was aware of it, they had reached the Lovers' Oak and seated themselves beneath its patriarchal boughs.

Lulie presently observed:

"Do you remember that love song you taught me a few weeks ago?"

Louis nodded.

"Suppose we sing it?"

"Just as you say, dearest."

Clasping each other's hands, the lovers sang
the following strain:

SHE AND I.

(Ballad.)

We were wooing in the starlight,
    She and I ;
We were bidding sweetest good-night
    'Neath the sky.
Ah, our hearts were wildly beating,
And the future dawned enchanting,
As our lips were pressed at parting.
    With a sigh!   *(bis.)*

We were at the altar kneeling,
    She and I ;
Angels from above were peeping
    To espy
And to watch love's flow'rets springing,
As we both began life's morning,
Anthems sweet and loving flinging
    To the sky!   *(bis.)*

We are seated in the starlight,
    She and I ;
We are speaking o'er life's days bright.
    Long gone by.
Though her tresses care has silver'd.
And my frame with age is fetter'd,
Still our love is deep and treasur'd
    Ne'er to die!   *(bis.)*

As the last echoes of the song finally died out, Louis heard a crackling noise behind him and started to his feet, filled with an undefined apprehension of danger. He glanced uneasily about, but seeing nothing unusual, resumed his seat.

"How nervous you are," exclaimed Lulie. "It must have been that same little rogue I was chasing a few moments ago. Talk love to me. All your poetry is so fervidly sweet, I am sure you can say such pretty things to the one who is dear to you."

Louis did not reply. In some inexplicable manner his thoughts had suddenly reverted to Yetta, and he regretted having so rashly betrothed himself to Lulie. He knew he could never care for her as he did for the strange girl who seemed to have mastered his very soul. Tears filled his eyes and he pressed his hand to his heart to stay its wild pulsations.

"What is the matter?" said Lulie, wonderingly. "I am sure I said nothing to make you feel sorry."

Louis clasped her to him.

"It is because I adore you above all things, that I act so strangely," he said, deliriously.

"Do you know what love is, blue-eyed angel?
It is the sublimest, the most princely gift of
God to mankind. It assuages grief, thrills the
whole world with happiness! By all I hold
sacred, I will do my best to make you happy.
You are a thousand times purer than those nun-
bred images, who come into the world to distress mankind with their lurid views of life."

Lulie looked at her lover with dilated pupils.

"How strangely you talk?" she said. "I
am almost afraid of you."

Louis kissed the wondering eyes and continued :

"You will be my treasured bride, sweet girl.
Here is to bind our hearts. It is the Alvez be-
trothal ring. Aye, it has never till this day been
the witness of such celestial love."

He put the heirloom around her finger. Her
head fell on his bosom and they remained for a
long time gazing into each other's eyes, whisper-
ing those tender nothings which only lovers
understand. Lulie suddenly started.

"How thoughtless of us," she said, fretfully.
"We will be late for supper and papa will scold.
I must run to my room and fix up. Kiss me,
quick."

Louis obeyed and Lulie ran down the path. She stopped when a few feet away, detached a rose which nestled in her hair, and threw it to him, saying:

"Keep this in memory of to-night."

Louis picked up the flower and placed it near his heart. As he did so, he heard the same noise which had aroused him while singing with Lulie. He looked furtively about and faintly made out the silhouette of a human form flitting between the trees. He started in pursuit, but the misleading twilight had now melted into the darker shades of night and he could no longer discern anything.

CHAPTER VII.

While my pulses thrill and quiver,
Thou shalt not enclasp another.

Louis felt nervous at the recurrence of the mysterious noise and remained for a long time lost in meditation.

"Pooh! it's only imagination," he reasoned; "my nerves are unstrung, and I would not be surprised to find a couple of ghosts waiting for me in my room."

He went to his apartment, refreshed himself,
and repaired to the sitting-room.   Yetta was
reading, but Lulie was not in her accustomed
place.   The young doctor glanced inquiringly
about.

" Miss Hevlin has retired to her room," observed Yetta, answering his look; "She does
not feel well to-night."

" Do you mean to say that Lulie is ill?"
asked Louis, anxiously.

" A slight indisposition," answered Yetta,
carelessly; "she probably caught cold in the
garden.   The air is quite chilly to-night.   This
will give you the opportunity of spending the
evening in my company, a luxury which you
have not enjoyed for a long time.   Sit beside
me and chat a little.   I am in high spirits to-
night."

She smilingly put aside her book.

" I thank you very much," said Louis, coldly;
"I prefer going to the club."

Yetta arose and placed a detaining hand on
his arm.

" Why are you so rude?" she reproachfully
said.   " It is no reason because we do not love

that we should be enemies for life. Let us be friends from to-night."

She looked pleadingly into his face. The young man's undefended heart was powerless against such an unexpected attack. The old love burned in his breast with frenetic ardor; Lulie was instantly forgotten.

"Let us sit on this sofa," said Yetta. "It is much more comfortable than those high-backed chairs."

Louis obeyed. Taking Yetta's hand in his, he tremulously said:

"Why do you care for my company to-night, Yetta? You who have been so cruel, so unrelenting in your harshness! Tell me, sweet girl, why your cheeks are as pink as roses and your eyes shine with unusual lustre to-night? Madcaps that we are to allow the golden hours to slip heedlessly by. Rest your head on my bosom, dearest, and tell me you adore me with as much fervency as I do you."

He passed his arm around her neck and drew her to him. For a moment she remained in his arms, then slowly freed herself.

"Do you love only me?" she asked, suddenly.

"I swear it," was the fond answer.

"And Lulie?"

Louis felt the blood receding from his face.

"Lulie?" he faltered.

"Yes, LULIE," emphasized Yetta, her eyes flashing. "If you love me only, why does the mere mention of that name frighten you?"

Louis had now regained his self-control.

"Well, that is a good one," he laughingly observed. "Jealous of that little blue-eyed doll-baby! I never gave her a moment's serious thought, dear. I was flirting with her just to tease you."

Yetta took up a small Bible near by and handed it to Louis, saying:

"Swear on this that you love me better than Lulie."

Louis raised the book to his lips.

"I swear—My God, look!"

The Bible fell to the floor and his senses reeled. He had suddenly caught sight of Lulie, who was seated near the door and gazing vacantly about, as if incapable of crediting her senses.

Yetta looked contemptuously at her lover.

"What new lies will you now invent," said

she, hotly. '' When she ran away from you and
you hypocritically pressed the rose she threw you
to your heart, I followed her, resolved to tell her
the truth. I asked her to come to my room after
supper and there I told her of your rascality.
She indignantly defended you, but I gradually
opened her eyes, and she tremblingly surrendered
the ring which only those of our blood have thus
far worn. Together we came to this room, and
when she heard your footsteps, I told her to
hide behind the door and she would see what a
knave you were. See how distracted she looks—
every word we uttered has pierced her trusting
heart. Go and soothe her with additional false-
hoods.''

She pushed him toward Lulie with such passionate force that he would have fallen had he
not steadied himself by grasping a chair. During Yetta's angry speech, Lulie had remained
immovable; she now pressed both her hands to
her heart, gave a choking sob and would have
fallen to the floor had not Louis caught her in
his arms.

'''Get a glass of water, Yetta, quick!'' he
cried, wildly.

Yetty glanced scornfully at him.

5

"You claim to be a doctor," said she; "you can spare my assistance." Then, changing her tone to one of exquisite sweetness: "You love me better than Lulie, do you not, Louis?"

She bent over him, a strange look in her eyes. His heart gave a great bound to meet her own and his whole frame quivered with emotion. He felt like abandoning Lulie and rushing into the arms of the girl he adored. But the nerveless hand resting in his felt so cold, the pallid face looked so pitiful, he turned his head away and said, in tones which involuntarily trembled:

"I wish you would stop this foolishness, Yetta. Give me a little help, and this poor girl will soon open her eyes."

He kissed Lulie's brow and caressingly smoothed her golden curls. Something flashed and he looked up to discover what it was. The sight which met his gaze froze his blood to icy coldness. Yetta stood staring at Lulie, her eyes aflame with unconcealed hatred, a bejeweled poignard in her hand.

Louis sprang to his feet.

"Yetta," he moaned, "are you mad?"

"It is not for *you*, coward," replied Yetta, pushing him aside.

She swiftly raised the poignard and attempted to plunge it into Lulie's bosom. Louis threw himself across the girl's body. The glittering blade pierced his breast a few inches below the heart, buried to the hilt. A mist passed over his eyes and he lost consciousness.

CHAPTER VIII.

"Thou hast called me thy angel in moments of bliss,
And thy angel I'll be, 'mid the horrors of this."

For months after the events narrated in the preceding chapter, Louis hovered between death and insanity. Night and day he raved about Yetta, imploring her to forgive him and begging her to come back to him. Sometimes he imagined that she relented and was bending over him with smiling lips, murmuring soothing phrases. When he held out his arms, her eyes would instantly flash with the fire of hate, she would become restless and menacing, and flee from him with a cry of horror.

When he finally recovered his faculties and was able to resume the practice of his profes-

sion, Louis was no more the flighty, debonair
youth of old. His features were care-worn
and sunken, his erst jet-black hair sprinkled
with gray, and an expression of settled sadness
glowered in his eyes.

Lulie was kind to the invalid during his con-
valescence, but gradually estranged herself
from him as he became stronger. She now
felt only indifference for the one she thought
she could love forever, and pitied him. Hers
had been a momentary passion—a young girl's
first love, and she experienced neither pain nor
regret that her dream had vanished.

No one spoke of Yetta and Louis dared not
mention her name. He had a vague premoni-
tion that the walls of St. Veronica Convent entombed her, and many were the anathemas he
heaped upon that institution.

One fateful day, while reading *Le Courrier
de la Louisiane*, Louis came across an article
headed "Taking the Veil," and carelessly
perused it. But something tugged at his heart
and the paper fell from his grasp when he
came to this paragraph:

"Among those who became the Brides of
Christ was Miss Yetta Delric, of this city.

She will be known in religion as Sister Dolores. The young lady is a niece of our eminent physician, Dr. Carlos Alvez."

"Lost forevermore!" Louis passionately cried. "O God! What have I done to be accursed with a hopeless love in the prime of life."

He buried his face between his hands and sobbed like a child.

"She is not lost to me," he exclaimed, rising. "Though I have to tear her away from the arms of those accursed nuns, she will yet be my bride."

He went to his desk and wrote a long letter to Yetta, beseeching her to grant him an interview. He bribed one of the maids employed about the Convent, who promised to deliver his message with the utmost secrecy and to bring an answer that same evening. She was faithful to her promise—but her message was verbal and conveyed the intelligence that Sister Dolores was lost to the world forever and sent her cousin a crucifix as a parting souvenir.

Louis recognized the little cross which had been a silent witness of his ardent vow to Yetta, and he dashed it to the ground. As he turned to go, he met the astonished gaze of his messenger.

"What the deuce are you gaping at?" he said, impatiently. "I thought you were miles away."

"I was waiting," was the sententious reply.

"Waiting for what? Am I still your debtor?"

"Monsieur will pardon me. I thought he wanted to *persevere.*"

She made a feint of going. A gleam of hope flashed across the horizon of despair.

"Wait," said Louis, eagerly. "You have given me an idea."

He drew forth the memorandum book in which he usually wrote his prescriptions and scribbled the following lines:

"YETTA—At half-past twelve to-night I will scale the wall of your convent and wait for you under the oak which stands a few feet from the entrance. If you do not meet me there, I will seek you in your cell.   LOUIS."

He folded this and handed it to the impassive girl, who all the time had kept her eyes fixed on the ground.

"Be careful that the nuns do not see this," he said, in admonitory tones.

"Monsieur can rely upon my discretion," replied the girl, bowing. She mechanically thrust the note into her bosom and was in the

act of walking away, when Louis detained her
with this remark:

"Are you also going to become a nun?"

The blue eyes flashed angrily.

"No, indeed; I hate them," was the un-
looked-for reply.

"You do not prove it," said Louis, laughing.

"On the contrary, Monsieur," answered the
girl, mischievously. "Do you think they would
feel glad were they to be apprised of what I am
doing for you? Ha, ha, ha! You do not know
all the tricks I play them."

She bowed effusively and walked off, merrily
singing one of Beranger's arias. Louis turned
his steps homeward with a hopeful heart, whist-
ling the tune his sprightly messenger was chant-
ing.

CHAPTER IX.

"They grieved, but no wail from their slumbers will come;
They joyed, but the tongue of their gladness is dumb."

The second week of December, 1826, promised to be a gala one for music-loving New Orleans. Two new plays were to be performed
for the first time at the Orleans Theatre: *The*

New Lord of the Village, by Favieres and Bey-
eldier, and *An Hour of Matrimony*, by Etienne
and Delayrac.   These were to be followed by
a one-act vaudeville from Scribe's prolific pen,
A Visit to Bedlam.

When the hour advertised for the beginning
of the performance drew near, every available
spot was filled by an expectant crowd; it seemed
that the whole city had turned out to do homage
to the triple bill.

A remarkable incident was noted by all and
commented upon in whispers with pro-
found amazement—young Dr. Alvez was
present! For the first time in many months
he was seen gaily chatting with the ladies,
exchanging witticisms with their escorts,
and criticising timely topics.   As the evening wore on, it was observed that he was
one of the foremost in encouraging meritorious
artists as well as the first to hiss whenever a
bad break was made.

When the curtain fell, Dr. Louis Alvez suddenly disappeared.   He had agreed to accom-
pany certain frolicsome young fellows to a
midnight supper with several feminine members
of the troupe, and was eagerly searched for—

but in vain. As his carriage was also missing, it was concluded that he had gone on a gallant adventure‘with a dashing soubrette he had vociferously applauded and clandestinely ogled whenever she appeared on the stage. Such feats were common among the gilded youth of those days and excited very little attention, except if it reached the ears of some doting mamma or jealous sweetheart, when the culprit would be severely reprimanded and only pardoned on his solemn promise not to sin again. Hence, the young doctor's convivial friends having reached the conclusion that he was perfectly satisfied, wherever he was, repaired gaily to the festal hall and soon forgot all about the absentee.

*   *   *   *   *   *

It lacked a few minutes to midnight. The motly crowd which had poured from the Orleans Theatre, half an hour before, highly pleased with the plays presented, had sought their respective homes—except those who made it a point, during the Carnival season, to seek repose only when night ushered morning. But the patter of hurrying feet, the whirring noise of the carriages and the indescribable tumult

incidental to such occasions, had died away, to
be revived the next night with the self-same
abandon and gayety.

Sixty-four years ago, our principal streets
were far from being the well-paved, brilliantly
lighted thoroughfares of to-day. Where arc
and incandescent lights now dazzle the sight,
were ungainly oil-lamps, swinging and creaking from the ends of cross-arms nailed upon
some convenient tree. As will be surmised,
this gave a very uncertain light, which was ex-
tinguished whenever an unusually frisky breeze
came whizzing around the corners.

The sidewalks were also very unreliable, being merely hardened ashes, oscillating planks
or—more often—the virgin soil, over which
pedestrians walked with doleful forebodings.
People seldom ventured out on foot after sun-
down, or, if they were compelled to do so, were
preceded by slaves carrying enormous lanterns.

On that special night, nearly all the lamps
had succumbed to the impetuous force of the
wind. The darkness was intense, objects being
undistinguishable a few inches distant. Un-
mindful of this cheerless aspect, a man hurried
along Esplanade avenue, guided by the feeble

rays of a sputtering lantern he held aloft. He
stumbled several times, but kept on with una-
bated energy. He soon reached Bourbon
street, into which he turned, and walked briskly
forward. When a few feet from Peace street,
his foot caught in the roots of a tree and he
was thrown violently to the ground, the lantern
dashing itself to pieces against the trunk of a
tree.* With some effort—for the fall had con.
siderably unnerved him—the wayfarer regained
his feet and proceeded with more caution, pressing his hand to his side and tottering like an
aged man.

Few would have recognized Louis Alvez in
that lagging figure—the youth who had been so
sprightly, so joyous, less than an hour before.
Aye! few could have identified that distorted-
colorless face to be the erst mirthful countenance
of the young doctor, whose presence had caused
so much excitement at the old Orleans Theatre,

Dr. Alvez had now reached the entrance
and stood before the frowning walls of St.
Veronica Convent, which loomed up like a
fortress. He looked about for a suitable place
to jump over, and was in the act of attempting

---

*A shattered lantern was found at this spot the day after Dr. Alvez's
disappearance. G. A.

the feat, when a light suddenly flared around the Union street angle of the wall. The ill-starred lover hastily clambered down and hid behind a tree.

"Some cursed patrolman making his rounds," he muttered. "Those nuisances are always prowling about when not needed."

The lantern was rapidly coming nearer and Louis apprehensively crouched in the shadow of the tree. Just as it was about to pass by, the light came to a standstill and he thought himself discovered.

"I can certainly make no tangible explanation of my presence," he resumed, placing a hand on the butt of his revolver. "I have suffered too much to be baffled. Good God, how my wound hurts to-night!"

He was about stepping from his concealment, when the lantern suddenly leaped into the air, described a semi-circle, and forthwith went out. A smothered "All right," came from within the enclosure, the gate noiselessly swung open, and a white form tripped out.

"At last, my Popotte!"

The voice belonged to the swinger of the lantern.

"How late you are, *mon bijou*," was the rat-
tling response. "Come, we must hurry. The
gay cavalier I was telling you about—Sister Dolores' beau—will soon be around, and we might
scare him. He is a good customer, and I don't
care to lose him. I wonder how he is going to
jump these walls, though? If he doesn't get
cut to pieces by the broken bottles, he'll surely
be caught by one of the traps. Ah, *mon cher*,
there will be a sensation worth talking about
when morning dawns. . . . What are you
loitering here for? Let us go. Re-light your
lantern, you clumsy darling!"

Louis recognized the French maid's voice.
The mysterious manœuvres of the lantern-bearer
were now clear: he was her lover, and the twain
were going off to some midnight masquerade.
Greatly relieved, the doctor stepped forward.
The young girl gave a startled cry and clung to
her companion, who would undoubtedly have
fled had she not resorted to this stratagem.

"Don't be afraid," said the intruder, re-
assuringly. "I simply want Popotte to unlock
that adamantine barrier for me. Be quick,
girl!"

Popotte glanced at her lover, who nodded

affirmatively without the least hesitation. The girl then unlocked the gate and Louis walked in. He heard the door creak as it swung shut again; Popotte's ceaseless babbling sounded fainter and fainter—he was now alone on the forbidden soil. He guardedly struck a light and looked at his watch. Twenty-five minutes past twelve! Surely, Yetta must be there. He peered eagerly about, but could discern nothing. He waited, and soon heard the half-hour bell tolling from the convent chapel. Still she did not appear. The three-quarter bell struck—no Yetta.

"It looks as if she wants to defy me," muttered Louis, pacing nervously about. "An Alvez never retrogrades."

He advanced resolutely toward the darksome building. A hand was laid on his arm and a voice he adored tremulously faltered:

"I am here, insane boy! Speak lowly or we will be overheard and the nuns will kill you— kill us both. I knew you were mad enough to carry out your threat and obeyed your summons. I—I—"

She burst into choking sobs. In a second, Louis was fondling her in his arms and the

beatings of her outspent heart once more confessed a love which ages could never obliterate.

They sought a bench near by, lest the nuns
should overhear them. They sat very close together, so close that Louis could feel her warm
breath fanning his cheek and see her eyes
shining through the gloom, like twin-stars on a
radiant night.

What mad things they must have murmured
on that fateful night! How blissful they must
have felt, huddled against each other, heedless
of the fleeting hours! It was only when they
heard the twitter of the birds and saw the darkness gradually blending with the whitish light
of morn that their thoughts returned to earth.

Louis pressed a fervid kiss on Yetta's lips.

"We must now part, my darling," he faltered.

The girl threw herself in his arms.

"Take me with you!" she cried, deliriously.
"I adore you more than my God—take me away
from this awful place, which fetters my body,
but can not restrain the leapings of my heart!
Let us seek some remote corner of the globe,
where you will make me your bride." She
stopped short and buried her face in her hands.
"No, no! that can never be," she moaned. "No

priest will marry a nun who has proved faithless
to her vows. Go, leave me to expiate the wrong
I did you."

She caught his head between her hands,
repeatedly kissed him, and darted away. He
sprang after her, but fell back with a groan.
In a moment, she was again beside him.

"I tell you we must part," she wildly exclaimed. "Be courageous, my—is—is this
blood?"

"My wound—has—broken—out," gasped
the youth. "Kiss—me—farewell,—Yetta."

He caught her hand to press it to his lips, but
it fell from his nerveless grasp. Yetta swiftly
drew a bejeweled poignard from her bosom,
ripped open her lover's garments, and tried to
stay the flow of blood with her hand. She felt
the heart-throbs becoming fainter and less regular, a slight tremor shook the pain-tossed
frame—all was over.

*   *   *   *   *   *   *

Popotte returned from her escapade half an
hour later. She noiselessly slipped in and was
horrified to see two bodies lying side by side
near the entrance. Her screams soon aroused
the nuns, who came trooping out like ghouls

and viewed with horrent hair the ghastly spectacle.

As a poignard was found buried in Sister Dolores' breast, it was surmised she had first stabbed her lover and then killed herself.

The bodies were buried within the Convent grounds, and to this day the young doctor's disappearance has been a conjectural mystery.

THE END.

LULETTE.

LULETTE.

CHAPTER I.

The widely-known cotton house of Margins & Co. had collapsed. Harold Mouques, who had but recently been promoted from clerk to chief book-keeper of the seemingly prosperous concern, found his air-castles totally demolished. He naturally felt moody and surly as he sat in his drawing-room the morning following the failure, glancing at the schedule of the firm published in the newspapers.

"I think I'll take Knouril's advice and turn my back on this city," he mused, half aloud. "I have a little cash laid aside and I might just as well lose it in the Old World."

He fumbled in his pocket and took out a letter, which he read carefully over. The concluding lines were thus:

"India is the best place for investing your capital just now. Look at me, for instance. Five years ago I came here with very little money; to-day I am the head of a firm known throughout the globe. The best thing you can do is to join me. I'll give you a cordial lift in memory of old days.   JOHN KNOURIL.''

Harold smiled contentedly and replaced the letter in his pocket. That same week, he made up his mind to follow his friend's advice, and before the end of the month was on his way to India. When he arrived at Calcutta, he had no difficulty in finding the house of Knouril & Co., famed throughout the world as dealers in precious stones, and was warmly welcomed by its chief.

Knouril's prosperous career read like a romance. A few years previously, he had suddenly left New Orleans, without even a word of parting to his friends. No explanations could be given for this strange freak. A few months afterward, he had written to his old college-mate, Harold Mouques, telling him of his arrival at Calcutta and vowing never to return to Louisiana. He gave no reasons for his action, and, although the friends had regularly · corresponded since, the mystery remained unsolved.

Shortly after his arrival, Knouril induced Harold to buy an interest in his firm. The

business prospered wonderfully, the two friends
finally buying out the other partners.

One morning Knouril seemed low-spirited
and uneasy, paying little attention to what
transpired about him. Upon being questioned
by Harold, he observed :

" I had a bad dream last night, old man."

" Is that all?" was the laughing remark.
" You are supersensitive this morning."

" I know it's womanish of me to be thus, but
I can't help feeling rattled. Evil is brooding
somewhere."

" What did you dream about?"

" Home," was the reply, given in such
pathetic accents that Harold glanced wonderingly at his friend.

" You seem surprised at my tenderness," resumed Knouril, sadly smiling.

" Of course I am. I thought you the most
unromantic man on earth."

" I have a heart, Harold. I thought it was
of marble, but the remembrance of a woman's
loving face sufficed to make its old wound bleed
afresh."

" What in the world are you talking about?"

Knouril drew a chair near his own and said:

"Sit here and I'll tell you all. You are my chum, my partner, and ought to know everything about my life. Do you remember how suddenly I left New Orleans?"

"Yes, especially when you had but recently graduated from the Tulane Medical College. Everybody said you were cranky at the time."

"Thanks. But let me tell you my story: As you may perhaps remember, I intended sailing for Europe to complete my studies with an uncle in Berlin, who is a man of note there. A few weeks before the time set for my departure, at a ball given at the Theatre de l'Opera, I met a young girl —the prettiest and most enthralling creature I had ever seen. I will call her Lulette. It was a case of love at first sight. I went wild over her; her eyes spoke her heart-thoughts. The day for my departure drew near. I formulated innumerable excuses for postponing same, but father positively refused to allow further delay. I insisted, and finally told him I would not go at all if he did not do as I wanted. We are a hot-headed family. Harold. When we desire anything, naught can turn us back. Father and I quarreled, he struck me—I retaliated. God forgive me, but it was not my fault."

He bowed his head and a tear coursed down his cheek.

"The rest is soon told," he resumed, with some effort. "The incident was carefully locked in our breasts and the world never heard of it. But I could not endure to face father day by day with the remembrance of that fatal blow gnawing at my heart. Without even telling Lulette—then my fiancée—farewell, I left the city of my birth and buried myself here. God knows I have suffered enough to atone for my sin."

Before Harold could frame a reply, a messenger rushed in and handed him a cablegram. He glanced at the superscription and said:

"It is addressed to you personally, John."

Knouril's face became as pale as a corpse.

"For Heaven's sake, tear it open and read," he groaned.

Harold obeyed. The contents were thus:

"*Come home immediately. Father dangerously ill. Asks for you.*

"MARCEL KNOURIL."

Knouril pressed both hands to his forehead and moaned.

"I knew it—I knew it," he said, in tones of pitiful despair.

"What are you going to do about it?" asked his sympathizing friend.

"The steamship leaves to-morrow; so do I."

CHAPTER II.

A month after Knouril's departure, his partner received the following note, hurriedly penned:

"DEAR OLD PAL: Pardon my reprehensible silence. To tell the truth, I am so happy I can think of nothing but Lulette. Just think of it, old man, we will be married next month! As I want you to dance at our wedding, leave the business in the hands of Letimlorn. He is competent and reliable in every respect. Fuller particulars when we meet.   JOHN."

"Not a word about his father," thought Harold. "I presume the old gentleman recovered, but John ought to have curbed his ecstacies for awhile to let me know how matters stood. Poor fellow! His head is completely

turned by his old love. Catch *me* getting luny
just because a woman smiles for me. Ugh!''

He curled his lips contemptuously and resumed his office duties. If he could only have
pushed aside the veil which hides the future
from mortal gaze!

Within a week, Harold settled the most im-
portant transactions of the firm and had the
necessary documents drawn up empowering the
head clerk of the house, Stephen Letimlorn, to
represent Knouril & Co. without reservation.
He then took passage on board a steamship
bound for Havre, which place he reached just
in time to engage a cabin on the *Fleur-de-Lys*,
the champion vessel of the French Transatlantic
Line, plying between Havre and New York.

On board the *Fleur-de-Lys* Harold became
acquainted with the charming Louisianian, Miss
Mirelle Arcos, whose final destination also
proved to be New Orleans. The young people
soon became fast friends, and, as the voyage
lengthened—well, it is the same, sweet, old
story.

The *Fleur-de-Lys* was a strongly built, iron-
plated steamship, under the command of Capt.
Alcide Ramie, an experienced French navigator.

She was the first iron merchant-vessel to cross the Atlantic and was considered the safest and fastest craft afloat.

Nothing of note happened until the coast of New Foundland was reached, where the vessel came upon a water-logged Norwegian barque. Capt. Ramie took care of her crew, who were nearly famished. The master of the barque reported having been wrecked by icebergs and warned the seamen to keep a sharp look-out.

Capt. Ramie burst into a hearty laugh at this caution.

"Icebergs?" he said, contemptuously. "This is not a bath-tub. Why, man, we can steam right through a mountain of ice as high and thick as the Great St. Bernard and come out unharmed!"

A boast which was assuredly-monumental, but the gallant tar spoke with such earnestness that the passengers and crew applauded unanimously.

The next day and the one following, the vessel steamed through numberless floes, which crashed and bumped against its iron sides. Huge icebergs were observed in the distance, but no one felt any apprehension. The *Fleur-*

de-lys was proof against such insignificant obstructions and kept on her course unfettered by their presence.

Evening came. A thick mist arose, enveloping the ship in a veil of impenetrable thickness. As regularly as the ticks of a faithful clock, the fog-whistle echoed its notes of warning, increasing in tone and frequency as the mist became thicker and more chilling.

" I've never seen such a fog since I've been on the Atlantic," remarked the Norwegian captain, as he gazed ominously around. " It is a bad sign, especially at this season of the year."

The passengers were all grouped about the deck when this remark was made. It had the effect of putting a sudden check to their laughing chats and each looked at the other in unfeigned apprehensiveness.

"Yes," continued the speaker, "a ship rarely reaches port under such circumstances. I've been navigating the seas for forty years, and know what I'am talking about."

He then proceeded to narrate innumerable yarns to prove his assertion and recited dismal passages from "The Ancient Mariner." There

was not a soul who felt comfortable when he
concluded. Even jolly Capt. Ramie, though
he kept on boasting of the immunity of his ship
from peril, looked ill at ease and paced the deck
with nervous foot-falls.

Miss Arcos and Harold remained outside for
a long time after the other passengers had retired, listening to the swashing of the waves and
the groaning of the ponderous machinery.

It was long after midnight when the lovers
separated.

CHAPTER III.

About half an hour after retiring to his
cabin, Harold awoke with a start and looked
wildly about. Everything was tranquil and he
turned over to resume his sleep. But this was
impossible. Every moment he would be startled by some noise or other and would sit up-
right in bed, fancying that the sea was already
swirling into his stateroom. Midnight tolled.
He softly arose, lit a match, and cautiously
opened the door. All was quiet, He crept
into bed, but could not sleep. At last, despairing of mastering his fears, he noiselessly slipped

out of the cabin and sought the sitting-room. It was deserted, but a cheery blaze flickered in the stove. He lit a cigar and sat beside the fire, smoking and dozing alternately.

"Crash!"

The huge ship quivered from bow to stern and Harold felt himself thrown to the floor, stunned, surprised, bewildered.

"Crash! C-r-a-s-h!"

A succession of terrific shakings, followed by the hissing of steam, the sounding of bells and gongs, and the shrill notes of the whistle of distress. The passengers rushed out of their staterooms and the scene became a veritable pandemonium. Men and women screamed and fought madly for the right of way; children wailed and were trampled unmercifully, smothered to death by the very ones from whom they sought succor.

Captain Ramie did superhuman efforts to quell the deadly stampede.

" Stop, you fools!" he yelled. " There's not the slightest danger. We only struck a small chunk of ice."

But his words were unheeded. He might just as well have tried to stop the inflow of the

icy waters, which were rapidly gaining the
mastery.

" Flash!"

The lurid signals of distress illumed the darkness for a few seconds, tinging the overhanging
clouds a dull red, death-boding hue.

" Boom! Boom?"

The cannons shrieked out their thunderous
affright, blending their noise with the groans of
the maddened mass of humanity. which struggled and squirmed about, hardly knowing what
they were doing.

" Hue-r-r-r-r-r! Rowr-r-r-r-r ru-r-r-r!"

The awful notes of the whistle of distress
stilled the beatings of the quavering hearts. But
it finally died out. The waters rushed in and
extinguihhed the fires; men and women fought
no more, but stood as if paralyzed. awaiting
their doom.

" I've been navigating the seas for forty
years." Harold heard a feeble voice gasp. " I
knew what I was talking about."

Just then the vessel gave a lurch, oscillating
like a boulder about to crash into an unfathomed
precipice, and the merciless waters swirled
about her. She stood still for a few seconds.

then plunged beneath the surface, carrying in
her wake the screaming mass, which despair-
ingly clung to the creaking timbers, imploring
in vain to be saved.

Harold felt himself going down, down, down
with frightful velocity; then he suddenly
stopped and was shot toward the surface. He
deliriously grasped at a floating piece of furni-
ture, and —

" I say, young gentleman, if you are not more
careful, you'll overturn that stove."

Harold glanced up and met the amused gaze
of Capt. Ramie.

" Where's Mirelle—tell me, quick—was she
also saved?" he gasped.

The old tar looked dubiously at the agitated
young man and made a dash for the sideboard.

" Here," said he, pulling out a bottle and
pouring some liquor into a glass. " Drink this
and you'll feel all right. It always demoralizes
a man to make love on a cloudy night."

Harold mechanically swallowed the beverage,
rubbed his eyes and looked dazedly about. A
bright fire burned in the stove; at his feet was
a half consumed cigar. The vibrations of the
ship's machinery kept on with the self-same

7

monotony. The shipwreck was only a dream!
He had fallen asleep haunted by the terrors of
the sea. and his imagination had evolved this
fantastic nightmare.

The ship reached New York in due time.
Harold and his fair protegé then took passage
on a steamship for New Orleans, which place
they reached without anything unusual happening. Having been informed of his friend's
coming, Knouril was waiting for him at the
wharf. He insisted on introducing the young
man at once to his adored Lulette. Remon-
strances were useless, and, in less than half an
hour after his arrival, Harold found himself in
the presence of Knouril's ideal, whose beauty
and sweetness he found had not been exagger-
ated by his friend.

It was only when the partners were once
more alone that Harold thought of John's father
and asked about him.

"Why, didn't I explain everything to you?"
queried Knouril.

"Certainly not. You raved about Miss Lulette—everything else was a blank."

Knouril burst into a hearty laugh.

"It was only a scheme to make me come

back," he exclaimed. "Father was at the theatre the night of my arrival. He treated the whole thing as a practical joke—and here the matter rests."

Harold gave his friend a heartfelt handshake and the pair separated.

A week afterward Lulette and John were married. Harold was best man, Mirelle his blushing companion. That same night, when he escorted her home, he obtained her promise that the next wedding at the old St. Louis Cathedral would be theirs.

In May, 1882, Harold and his bride left New Orleans for India, which they decided to make their future home. Lulette feeling saddened at the thought of leaving her native land, Knouril abandoned his idea of returning to Calcutta and left his partner in full charge of the business of Knouril & Co.

And, following the diction of the dear old fairy tales which delighted us in our youths, may the lovers live in happiness to the end of their lives.

THE END.

IRRECONCILABLE.

IRRECONCILABLE.

"O, why should the spirit of mortal be proud?
Like a swift-fleeting meteor, fast-flying cloud,
A flash of the lightning, a break of the wave,
Man passes from life to his rest in the grave."--*Knox.*

Some sections of the French quarter of New
Orleans have of late undergone noticeable
changes. Damp, ivy-twined dwellings, built
during the Spanish domination of Louisiana,
have been demolished and handsome stores and
cottages erected in their stead.

Many will recall a certain quaint, stately edi-
fice on Royal street, a few squares from
Esplanade avenue, which not long ago occupied the site where a vast dry goods establishment now stands. The process of demolition
was commenced about a year ago and now, as
one admires the elegant building which has so
rapidly replaced its predecessor, the sudden
change is always a subject of wonder to him.

A few months after the workmen had begun

razing the old building, a secret cabinet was discovered, in which were several chairs, a lounge and two old-fashioned book-cases. Everything was deeply covered with dust, and when the mouldy rags scattered over the lounge were removed, a skeleton rattled to the floor. A rusty pistol, with one chamber empty, was found near by. The newspapers, too busy with the bitter political fight then raging, treated the matter lightly, merely mentioning the strange find in their local columns. The bones were taken in charge by the coroner and buried in Potter's Field.

The writer not long since had occasion to transact some business with the contractor who erected the modern building—a well-known Creole gentleman—and was told of the unearthing of the skeleton.

" I always wondered why the press did not make a big sensation out of this," observed the narrator. " I could have furnished them startling details, father having told me the strange story connected with this old house. Many old-timers still recall the crazed father's irrevocable vow and his unexplained disappearance."

When pressed for a full recital, he laughingly said:

"My dear boy, I'm too busy. Come and take breakfast with me Sunday and I'll unbosom myself."

He kept his word and furnished the basis for this touching romance, which is given with faithful adherence to reality.

* * * * * * *

About half a century before the present generation was born, there lived in that historic Royal street residence a family by the name of Mizaine, consisting of father, mother, daughter and a spinster relative.

Major Hamilcar Mizaine was a survivor of the Battle of New Orleans, where his gallantry had cost him an arm. Having amassed a fortune on his sugar plantation in St. Charles parish, he had disposed of it at a handsome profit and moved to his native place, to live in ease and elegance.

To those whom he liked, the Major was a valued friend, but his sensitive nature resented the slightest affront. As an illustration of his unforgiving disposition, the following incident is related:

When attending college, one of his professors, vexed by some insolent remark, boxed his ears.

"I am only sixteen and powerless," warned the furious boy, "but when I become a man, I will make you regret your cowardice."

Every one laughed heartily at this bravado, but the youth resolutely carried out his threat. On the anniversary of his twenty-first birthday, he sought the professor, then still in the prime of life, and publicly slapped his face. A duel followed, in which Mizaine sent a bullet through his adversary's heart.

The Major's wife, whose maiden name was Pauline Oursblanc, was one of those cold, indifferent, unapproachable characters fortunately so rare among the descendants of the Franco-Latin race. She was too indolent to look after her sole child, sweet, timid Juanita, and had left her in the entire care of her sister-in-law, Cecile, who had proved a real mother to the girl.

Amid such surroundings, it was not surprising that Juanita did not feel for her parents those tender sentiments of love and respect which kindness fosters in an immature breast. Her father frowned upon her childish demonstrations of joy; her mother never kissed her babbling lips or tenderly spoke to her. "Aunt Cecile" was the only one in that dismal household who seemed to love her, and to her the child confided all her joys and sorrows.

Cecile had given her niece the best preceptors, and at fifteen she was more learned than the average girl of the period—for at that time the education of women was considered unimportant—and gave indications of soon blooming into a beautiful creature. She was one of those delightful caprices of nature, a blonde Creole, and her pretty face was the envy of her schoolmates and the pride of her aunt.

In those days it was customary to marry young, and Mme. Mizaine suddenly discovered she had a daughter old enough to think of beaux. So she nonchalantly remarked one day during breakfast:

"It is time you should think of marrying, Juanita."

Startled by the suddenness of the question, the young girl opened her blue eyes to their fullest capacity.

"Marrying?" she repeated, in surprised tones, "Why, I never loved any one!"

"Love is nonsensical, child." was the lymphatic response. "Had I married for love, I would be an old maid to-day."

The Major looked up amusedly at this frank admission, but said nothing. Mme. Mizaine continued:

"I will give a soiree in a few months to introduce you to society. In the meanwhile, Cecile will instruct you how to behave in company."

Juanita looked apprehensively at her mother, afraid to make any observation, and the meal was finished in silence.

On her sixteenth birthday, Juanita made her initial bow to society. She had winning manners, was an excellent pianist, and conquered many hearts that eventful night. But her sweetest smiles and most coquettish looks were bestowed upon Senville Faibus, a rich, handsome young fellow, who was considered a splendid "catch" by scheming mothers. Mme. Mizaine smiled encouragingly, for in her eyes Senville was a desirable suitor and would undoubtedly make a pliant son-in-law. As for the Major, he cordially toasted the young man at supper and invited him to call as often as he desired—a departure from his usual surliness which elicited general wondering comment.

As the weeks went by, Senville became bolder and more demonstrative in his attentions, completely routing his numerous rivals. One evening, when he had been unusually tender and had departed with unconcealed reluctance, Mizaine patted Juanita's blonde curls and pleasantly said:

"This is splendid, my child! I am really proud of you!

Juanita looked up in speechless amazement. Ever since she was a child, she could not recollect such a warm proof of paternal love.

"Yes," continued the Major, "I am delighted with you. Flirt as much as you please, but do not go *too* far."

"What do you mean, father?" said the bewildered girl, made uneasy by his caressing touch.

"I mean that Senville can be your toy as long as you please, but your husband—never."

"Father! I thought you liked him so much?"

"He is a pleasant young fellow, but you are too young to love sincerely. You will change your mind and make him suffer. I watched him closely to-night and I know he will adore you forever."

Juanita cast down her eyes. What could all this mean? He was surely jesting.

"But father," she ventured, timidly, "I do not understand why you do not want us to marry. I am old enough to love truly and I feel I can never forget Senville."

The Major's features grew sombre.

"I tell you this is all nonsense," he said. "Make him crazy, drive him wild, but bear in mind that you can never marry him."

"But I do love him dearly, father. How can—"

"Love has no existence at your age. You may suffer a little, but you will forget and be happier later."

In vain Juanita pleaded—Mizaine was inexorable. Exasperated by the girl's earnestness, he finally said :

"Enough of this nonsense. If you disobey me, may my eternal curse rest on you, your husband, your children and everything dear to you."

He walked away in a towering passion.

Juanita disconsolately sought her aunt and told her all. The good soul consoled her and explained what she thought prompted her brother to hate Senville.

"Senville's father and Hamilcar were classmates and inseparable friends." she began, tenderly kissing the tear-wet cheeks. "When your father was twenty-two, he fell desperately in love with Essie Burtel, a beautiful American girl. She accepted him and everything was in preparation for the wedding, when she ran away with young Faibus. Hamilcar was frantic with grief and rage and vowed revenge. Everybody expected a duel to the death, as both men were brave and reckless, but your father did not seek a hostile meeting. Soon after, he married Pauline and his wound was thought to be healed. Do you now understand. my child?"

Juanita arose, her bosom heaving with emotion.

"Yes, I now see it all." she said indignantly. "Father thought I would jilt Senville, thus punishing him for his mother's falsity. But I will do no such thing. He has never shown a father's solicitude for me and I defy his curse. I *will* marry Senville."

"Juanita!" exclaimed Cecile, alarmed at her impetuous words.

The poor girl threw her arms around her neck and kissed the withered cheeks.

"Dear. sweet, darling aunt." she sobbed. "you are the only one who really cares for me."

* * * * *

A few nights after the above conversation took place, Senville found Juanita alone in the garden, and confessed his love. She tremulously told him of her father's terrible words. Senville was dazed.

"God is too just to hearken to such vows," he said. "If you love me, we will be happy. But I do not ask you to disobey your father if your heart dictates otherwise."

She circled her arms around his neck.

"Yes. God is too good to blame us." she said, simply. "I love you and nothing can tempt me to make you feel unhappy."

He kissed her quivering lips and her anguished heart was solaced.

* * * * *

The elopement of Juanita Mizaine and Senville Faibus created quite a stir in social circles. Senville's parents could give no explana

tion to the innumerable questions propounded
to them and looked upon the affair as "a romantic escapade of two young fools." To
those bold enough to question the Major, he
invariably replied:

"My daughter is dead and buried. I do not
care to discuss the subject."

Two years after their elopement, the young
people returned to New Orleans, bringing a
little stranger with them—called by the sweet
name of Micaëla—whose fair face was so much
like Juanita's that she needed no formal .intro-
duction to establish her relationship to that
happy young woman.

Juanita tried to communicate with her parents, asking their forgiveness, but her advances were repulsed. Cecile was dead, thus
depriving the girl of the only relative who
would have welcomed her.

For three years the young people were very
happy. Then came a sudden change. The
bank in which was deposited the fortune of the
Faibus family—an institution which had with-
stood financial crashes for nearly a century—
collapsed, leaving Senville penniless. It was
then he felt the glamour of money. Former

8

friends, who fawned around him when fortune's star was in its zenith, now greeted him with coldness and arrogance, and refused assistance. To support his wife and child, he was compelled to work with common laborers on the river front; but this proved too arduous for him and he soon sickened and died. For her child's sake, Juanita wrote a suppliant letter to her father. She received the following answer:

" You are an impostor. My only daughter is dead."

The young widow then found employment in a manufacturing establishment. One day, sundry articles were missed, and, being the poorest employé, suspicion naturally rested upon her and she was discharged.

" You may thank your stars we do not send you to jail," said the superintendent, sternly. " The balance we owe you is insignificant to cover your thefts, but we will be lenient and give you a chance to reform."

Poor Juanita! Her baby—now a prattling, intelligent child of six—had been feverish all night and she was waiting for her week's wages to buy some medecine and toothsome tid-bits. With a despairing heart she sought her wretched

home. Micaëla's face became radiant when
she saw her mother.

" I thought you would never come, mamma,"
she said, caressing the pallid cheeks. " I'm
so hungry."

Juanita passionately kissed the bright eyes.

" And what delicacy does my precious want
to-night?" she said, laughing boisterously to
conceal her agitation.

Micaëla was pensive a few moments.

" I feel so much like eating nic-nacs and
milk," she observed longingly. " That good
colored woman next door gave me some this
morning and it did me such a heap of good."

Juanita fumbled in her purse and found—five
cents! Aye, even this simple luxury was denied the little sufferer. A desperate resolve
overmastered her pride.

"I can not allow my baby to die," she thought;
"I will seek father and compel him to take care
of her. He may have no compassion for me,
but he must save this innocent life."

The air being cool and the weather drizzly,
she wrapped a shawl around the little fevered
form and tottered out of the room.

A grand ball was in progress in the spacious

Mizaine parlors. The Major had just been elected to Congress and was honoring his constituents. As he passed through the hallway the door leading into the street cautiously opened and an anxious, frightened face peeped in.

"What the mischief do you want?" he gruffly queried, opening the door.

But he started, for an appealing face was raised to him and a choking voice faltered:

"Have mercy, father! Your grandchild is dying. Abuse me, but save her life."

The old man turned as pale as a corpse. In spite of her faded dress and emaciated features, he had recognized his daughter! For a few moments he gazed vacantly at her, unable to speak. Then memories of the past surged through his brain, and he recalled his fateful vow. Recovering his wonted calmness, he coldly said:

"You have come to the wrong house, madam. My only child died seven years ago."

He slammed the door in her face and joined the impatient revelers. That same night he disappeared and was never heard of again.

The next morning an unconscious woman, tightly clasping the dead body of a child, was found by the police in a doorway on Royal street, a few doors from Major Mazaine's residence.

The unfortunate creature was taken to the Charity Hospital, where kind hands ministered to her, but aid had come too late and she died before sunset. No one identifying her, she was buried by the city.

* * * * *

The discovery of a skeleton in the old Spanish building clears away the mystery surrounding Major Mizaine's disappearance. Gnawed by remorse, he had sought this secret spot and put an end to his misdirected life. This theory is rendered irrefutable by the finding of an unloaded pistol near the ancient lounge.

May God have mercy on the poor bones lying uncared for in a pauper's grave!

THE END.

THE

CREOLE FLOWER GIRL.

THE CREOLE FLOWER GIRL.

—

CHAPTER I.

At the beginning of this century, in the neighborhood of that world-famed relic of colonial New Orleans, the French Market, there used to be an attractive flower shop, presided over by a bright-eyed little brunette. She was a charming beauty, full of wit and tact, and did a thriving business. Although very amiable and talkative, she was mysteriously reserved about her personality, no one knowing her real name or antecedents. To those indiscreet enough to question her, she gave evasive answers, and no amount of coaxing could induce her to become confidential.

Ernest Fatah was her best and most assiduous customer. His heart had been stolen since the day those delicate fingers pinned a *boutonnière* for him, but his advances having been coldly received, he consoled himself with the thought that he could at least see her every morning.

Young Fatah was a reporter on the only newspaper then existing in New Orleans—*Le Courrier de la Louisiane.* He was a popular sketch-writer and versifier, most of his work appearing in the *Courrier.*

One morning, he met his ideal as she was coming out of the St. Louis Cathedral, and smilingly approached her.

"Do you object to my company as far as your residence," he said.

"Oh, I am not bound for home," was the disappointing response. "I am simply going to visit a sick friend. You may walk with me as far as her door, if you wish."

Ernest's beaming features showed the three last words to be surplusage.

"You are a mystery to me Mademoiselle," he said, a puzzled expression on his handsome face. "Once I asked you to tell me a little of your life and you seemed unaccountably displeased. Why are you so unkind? You know it is not a spirit of curiosity which prompts me to—"

" Please do not begin again, I entreat you," interrupted the girl, "I know you are an honorable gentleman and I admire your discretion, but I can not tell you more than you already know. It is useless to plead Mr. Fatah."

The young man gave a start of surprise.

"Why, do you know my name?" he said.

The young girl looked confused, but frankly replied:

"You will pardon my curiosity, but you seemed such a quiet gentleman and took my refusal to receive you at my house so philosophically, that I made it a point to ascertain your name. It is a habit I have to know who my regular customers are."

Ernest glanced at her, but she averted his gaze.

"As you know my name," he convincingly said, "would you deem it bold if I asked yours?"

"Not at all, sir," was the quick reply. "I am Mayoutte, the Creole Flower Girl. I thought you knew it. Everybody calls me thus."

There was such an innocent look in her lustrous eyes, Ernest's rising displeasure was dispelled.

"I know your *given* name," he said, softly;

" but you surely have another—a family name, miss."

" Perhaps I once did, but I do not recall it."

" You are jesting. One can see by your conversation and manners that you are not plebeian. Your answer is incomprehensible."

" There are stranger things in this world, Mr. Fatah. Were you to know my past life you would wonder how I could apparently be so volatile and gay. One day I might tell you. For the present, I rely on your honor not to question me. We must now part, as I have reached my destination. Au revoir, sir."

Ernest walked regretfully away, more determined than ever to know the true history of this mysterious girl. The next morning as he stopped for his customary bouquet, Mayoutte seemed less gay than usual.

" What has happened to the queen of flowers," he observed pleasantly.

Mayoutte pointed to the clouded sky.

" The sun has not given her its morning kiss," she said laughingly. Then, looking graver: "You must not mind me, Mr. Fatah. Once in a while thoughts of the past trouble me and I grow despondent. To-morrow you will find me as of old."

" If it was not a forbidden subject," said Ernest, hesitatingly, " I would ask a few questions."

Mayoutte glanced into his love-lit eyes, but instantly averted them.

" Do not look at me that way," she said nervously.

Ernest feigned to be vexed.

"If even my looks are hateful to you," he stiffly said, "it would be more chivalrous to leave you alone. I trust you will pardon my intrusion, Miss."

He bowed and walked toward the door. His ruse was successful, for a detaining hand was placed on his arm:

" Do not be angry, Mr. Fatah," was the gentle remark. " I did not mean to offend you. You have been too kind to be treated with ingratitude."

Ernest saw his advantage and persuasively said:

" Be more friendly, cruel girl. Your bright eyes have surely read my heart's secret."

" Do not talk that way," said Mayoutte, apprehensively. " We might be overheard."

"Impossible," cautioned Ernest. "This little corner is too removed from the street."

"It is best to be prudent. When we are certain not to be overheard, I will speak fearlessly."

Ernest's heart gave a bound.

"This may never happen, unless — "

He stopped, and their eyes met again.

"I will do as you wish, Mr. Fatah," said Mayoutte, lowly. "I do not know how it is, but I feel so strange when you look at me that way. I—I do not like it. If I allow you to visit me, will you promise on your honor never to speak of love to me, unless I tell you to?"

Ernest looked perplexedly at her.

"Do you refuse? It is the only alternative."

She spoke firmly, but her voice quavered a little. Concealing his almost uncontrollable happiness, for the girl's heart-thoughts were mirrored in her reproachful eyes, Ernest indifferently said:

"I agree to respect your wishes, Miss Mayoutte. When may I call? Would this evening be too soon?"

Mayoutte hesitated and then hastily scribbled on a small slip of paper.

"Here is my address," she said uneasily.
"Act as your conscience dictates. Please go
now. I am afraid people will gossip about us."

Ernest took the precious document and departed. But he pondered for a long time over
Mayoutte's singular phrase: "*Act as your conscience dictates.*" He felt he loved her sincerely and would make her his wife if the story of
her life proved her to be as pure as he imagined, and he wondered what she meant. The
mystery was becoming more bewildering than
ever, and he felt a pang at his heart when he
thought how tediously long the day would be.

CHAPTER II.

The sun's last rays were tinting the sombre
clouds as Ernest stopped before Mayoutte's
residence and softly raised the quaint iron
knocker. The gate being half-opened and no
one responding to his knock, he walked into
the garden-path which led to the house and
looked musingly about. Roses, dahlias, mig-

nonettes and bright-colored tropical flowers bloomed in the open air, distilling a delicious fragrance. As he strolled toward the house, the door was suddenly opened and Mayoutte appeared on the threshold.

She was indeed a lovely creature. Of medium height, slender, with large black eyes and a magnificent wealth of chestnut hair, she was well calculated to excite admiration from the most prosaic. And as Ernest did not even remotely belong to this latter class, being a poet and dreamer, his state of mind can better be imagined than described. Mayoutte smiled at his confusion and observed:

"Come in, Mr. Fatah. You will catch cold standing on the damp soil so long. You are earlier than I expected."

She seemed so graciously unconscious of his embarrassment, that Ernest came to his senses.

"I was admiring your pretty flowers," he said. "I hope you will pardon my abstraction."

He took her proffered hand and they entered the house.

Seeing the young girl was so merry, Ernest

did not broach the subject of his visit, but employed his time in subtle assaults upon her undefended heart.

"I read a very pretty poem by you in the *Courrier* last Sunday," observed Mayoutte, after a pause in the conversation.

"You are very charitable, I am sure," said Ernest. "I am delighted to see I had an approving critic."

"Oh, I always read your poetry with pleasure. Before I knew you I always looked for it in the *Courrier* and was disappointed when you slighted a number. How is it you always sing of love?"

"It is such a sublime—"

But Mayoutte's warning finger stopped him.

"Take care," she said, playfully. "Do not venture too rashly on the quicksand of poesy."

"You are despotic, Miss Mayoutte. You push me temptingly near the illusive goal and then blame me for falling in."

"I spoke of your poetry, sir," she scoldingly responded.

"Are you afraid I might become personal?"

9

"Yes. I know how impetuous you poets
are. Once started, an avalanche can not stop
you."

"But a woman will," said Ernest, teasingly.
"In that case your sex should be more dreaded
than—than—I should like to know what you are
laughing at, Miss?"

"I was just thinking how courageous you
were, Mr. Fatah."

Ernest bit his lip.

"Now you are angry," resumed Mayoutte,
apologetically. "To atone for my offence, I
will ask you to write a verse or two in my al-
bum. Poetry is an infallible cure for rebellious
thoughts."

"Especially when it has a congenial subject," ventured Ernest.

They sat around a table and Ernest began
inditing. Now and then he would glance at
Mayoutte for an inspiration, but she seemed
deeply interested in the texture of her dress and
did not once raise her eyes. At last the poem
was finished and he placed the open book before
her.

"Read it aloud," she said. "It will seem
nicer."

Ernest read as follow:

THE POET TO HIS SWEETHEART.

When your eyes are upturned to my face, hallowed
    love,
The bright worlds which glimmer so grandly above
        With envy soon fade:
When your rosy lips part, fondest phrases to tell,
The harpists celestial their rhapsodies quell
        To listen, fair maid.

You are sweet as the rose by the South wind caressed
And your throat is as white as the proud lily's crest;
        Your heart pure as snow
Which vigilant guardians of Heaven elude.
When beside me you sit sorrows dare not intrude
        And woes blissful grow.

L'ENVOY.

Rise, fond tide of my heart, to the being I prize,
On the billows of Fate, like the sea to the skies,
        When she smiles to my call!
Hide thy pale rays, O Sun! Jealous moon disap-
    pear!
Angels, stay with the stars when this maiden draws
    near—
        She is fairer than all!

"It is quite pretty," said Mayoutte, "but it
is only a poetical conceit? You do not mean
it?"

"Of course not," answered Ernest, decisively. "I remember my promise too well to be guilty of actually thinking such things."

But his looks said otherwise, and Mayoutte became once more furiously interested in that tantalizing dress.

"May I return this book to the mantelpiece?" said Ernest, taking this as a pretext to make her look up.

"Certainly," replied Mayoutte, without glancing at him.

He walked briskly as far as the chimney and then came back on tip-toe and stood behind Mayoutte. She slowly raised her head to see where he was and he noticed a tear trembling on her lashes. In an instant, she was caught in his arms and he was tenderly kissing her moistened eyes.

"Oh, sir, please leave me go!" she pleaded, struggling to free herself. "What will you think of me now!"

"I love you, dearest," said Ernest. "Tell me you care for me."

"No, I hate you," was the sobbing response. "I thought you were a gentleman and extended you the hospitality of my home and now you insult me! Our friendship ends to-night, Mr.

Fatah. Oh, how *could* you take advantage of a lone, unhappy woman!"

She cried as if her heart would break and Ernest began to fear she would be overheard.

"Do not be so cruel," he gently remonstrated. "I love you and will make you my wife. Say you approve me, sweet girl."

Mayoutte dried her tears and sadly remarked:

"You have read my heart and wish to know why I can not requite your love. I warned you not to think of me otherwise than as a friend, but you did not heed me. I will tell you the truth, Mr. Fatah. I am married."

Ernest's face became ashy and he sprang to his feet.

"What?" he cried, fiercely.

But the beseeching eyes calmed his anger and he resumed his seat. He hardly gave credence to such an astonishing confession.

" Mayoutte," he presently said, " you are a Modern Sphinx to me. You have an attractive home; you are endowed with more accomplishments than the average girl of the period, yet you are not happy. Another thing which puzzles me: Why do you sell flowers when you

could easily fill a more lucrative and exalted
calling?''

" Why do I sell flowers?'' repeated Mayoutte,
dreamily. '' I hardly know. I like to be in-
dependent and I find consolation in my flowers.
They are never unkind, and I love them.'' She
was lost in thought for awhile. '' I was too
impulsive in judging you, Mr. Fatah,'' she resumed. '' I am to blame. I should never have
been weak enough to make our friendship
stronger. But it is too late now and as I do not
wish you to think ill of me, I will tell you the
story of my life.''

'' That is why I am here to-night,'' said
Ernest. '' You seemed so gay when I came, I
did not wish to make you feel sad by alluding
to the subject. Tell me all. I am certain
nothing terrible shadows your pure life.''

They returned to the sofa and Mayoutte began, hesitatingly at first, but becoming more
confidential as she proceeded:

''You were right in thinking me of good
birth. My true name is Josefa de Aillieres.
My parents still live on our estates in the Attakapas and my ancestors, as history has no doubt
informed you, rendered gallant services to

poor France before the Reign of Terror ensan-
guined her standard. But father fortunately
escaped the horrors of the Revolution, as he emi-
grated to Louisiana about 1768, exactly fifty years
after New Orleans was founded. He married
a few years afterward. I was his eighth child
and the only one who survived the terrible
epidemic of 1785. I lost five brothers and two
sisters within three months. Three died the
same day. I was then nearly a baby, but I
vividly recall that fearful day—those three
coffins ranged side by side and the grief of my
parents.* Oh, Mr. Fatah, it was awful!"

She placed her handkerchief to her face and
sobbed. Ernest's eyes were moist and he felt
a choking sensation in his throat, but controlled
his emotion and gently comforted the girl. She
gradually became calmer and resumed:

"Years went by without anything eventful
happening. One day—about five years ago—
father brought a stranger to spend a few weeks
with us. He was a Northern speculator and
was looking for an investment in Louisiana
lands. He appeared to be a man of means and
refinement, was handsome and intelligent, and

---

*A historical fact. G. A.

I fell in love with him. He seemed very fond
of me, but father considered me a mere child
and laughed heartily when I told him the
Northerner had asked me to become his wife.

" ' He was making fun of you, you romantic
little goose,' he said. ' Run to your room;
your dolls are crying for you.'

" When I told this to my suitor, he said he
would speak to father that same evening. He
did so, but was chilly received.

" ' I can give you no definite answer, sir, '
I overheard father saying. ' I have much
friendship for you, but I know nothing of your
antecedents. We old Frenchmen are very
strict on that score. You were introduced to
me by my broker and I asked no questions, not
having a marriageable daughter—for Josefa is
only fifteen. I do not refuse the honor you
wish to confer upon me, but furnish me proper
credentials and I will act accordingly.'*

" I thought this was quite unkind of father,
my suitor seeming such a perfect gentleman,
and I admired the dignified way in which he
took his rebuff. He was sad and pensive when

---

*This may seem odd to the present generation, but it was the laudable
and invariable rule of the old Creoles not to entertain anybody. Good
credentials were indispensable. G. A.

he met me in the drawing-room and I had not the
courage to refuse when he asked me to walk
about the garden with him. He then told me he
was going in the morning, never to return. He
loved me, but respected father's antagonism to
Americans and did not want to thrust himself in
a family where he was not liked by all. He
talked long and earnestly and completely turned
my head. I agreed to elope with him, and the
next morning abandoned those who had been
so kir . to me to please a total stranger. It was
the usual sequel, Mr. Fatah. He took me to
Philadelphia, where we lived happily for a year.
One morning he abandoned me, leaving a letter
in which he told me I had better go back to my
parents and allowing me enough money to do
so. I came as far as New Orleans, but had not
the courage to seek those I had so cruelly
wronged. Alone and friendless, I did not
know what to do, and so rented this littte cot-
tage and opened a flower stand. I first felt
humiliated and was shy and nervous, but little
by little I accustomed myself to my surroundings and to-day I take my fate philosophically."

"Have you never heard from your husband?" kindly observed Ernest.

"I do not even know if he exists. You now understand why we can not be happy, Mr. Fatah?"

"If your husband were dead," said Ernest, expectantly, "would you marry me?"

He read the answer in her tear-wet eyes and resolved to do all in his power to bring back their happy light.

CHAPTER III.

Ernest quietly instituted inquiries concerning the de Aillieres and soon secured an introduction to that influential Acadian family. Although he longed to speak of the subject which monopolized his thoughts, he deemed it best to be patient and observe a little. He had come ostensibly to "write up" the country and seek material for character sketches. Being of French descent, he was hospitably entertained. His affability soon won the friendship of the good-hearted people and he was told the odd folk-lore and legends of the Attakapas region, which he treasured in his memorandum book for publication in the *Courrier*.

One evening, after Mrs, de Allieres had
been unusually reminiscent, she sadly observed :

"Our own family has also had its sad romance, :
Mr. Fatah. It is a subject which is never al-
luded to here, but which still causes our hearts
to pang."

Ernest could hardly restrain his excitement.

" Would you think me intrusive if I asked a
recital?" he said.

" Not at all, sir. I have confidence in your
discretion."

She then told him the story of Mayoutte's
flight with the Northerner, stopping now and
then to wipe away a tear.

" You never knew what became of the poor
girl?" queried Ernest, a suspicious tremor in
his voice.

" We did all we could to find her, but to no
avail," was the answer. " The wretch who
wronged us probably killed her."

" No, madam, your daughter is not dead,"
said Ernest, forgetting his restraint. " You
shall soon see her."

He spoke with such assurance, the old

lady seized both his hands and imploringly said :

"Oh, sir, do not keep me in suspense? Tell me everything, whether good or bad.''

Ernest obeyed, repeating the story he had heard from Mayoutte's tremulous lips. * * * The next day, Mr. and Mrs. de Aillieres, accompanied by the young journalist, left for New Orleans.

There are happenings in our lives which defy the pen of the chronicler. However ambitious he may be, his ideas become confused and sterile, taking life and dying in the same breath. The heart beats in unison with the event which affects it, the eyes become moist, the bosom oppressed, but the romancer's individuality is lost and he imagines himself a real actor in the scene he yearns to depict.

Such were the feelings which overmastered the writer when he attempted to portray the meeting between Mayoutte and her joyful parents. Aye, the pen he wields is not eloquent enough to describe this touching reconciliation and give life to the expressions of unfettered delight which escaped the lips of those three mortals.

Josefa—for she is no more to us Mayoutte, the Creole Flower Girl—followed her parents to their Acadian home. At his fervid solicitations, she consented to correspond with Ernest, her parents agreeing thereto.

A year elapsed. Every five or six weeks Ernest would receive a friendly letter from Josefa. There were no mail-routes in those days, correspondence being carried on by means of couriers, and four weeks was considered a remarkable feat in the transmission of a letter from the interior. What a contrast to the present lightning-like mail trains? But this was nearly a century ago; one hundred years hence an inflated generation will mock what we now highly prize and deem indispensable.

One day Ernest received a cheerful—almost loving—letter from Mayoutte, in which was this simple postscript:

"If you can spare the time, come and see me."

These mysterious words puzzled the young man not a little. There was only one solution —a personal explanation with the one who framed them. As luck would have it, a planter from Grand Coteau was returning home that same evening and was delighted to have "somebody to talk to" during his tedious journey.

Ernest was cordially welcomed by the de Aillieres. Josefa did not conceal her gladness at seeing him again, and seemed unusually tender and attentive. In the evening, when the family was grouped for a friendly chat around the crackling log wood fire, Josefa handed the young man a newspaper clipping, bidding him to read it.

"It was not from your pen," she said, in a low tone, "but it lightened my sorrowful heart."

The printed slip read as follows:

"A letter from Philadelphia to Commagere & Co., of this city, brings news of the suicide of Warren Proctor, the well known broker. Financial ruin is the assigned cause for the deed. Deceased was unmarried."

"I read that in the *Courrier* weeks ago, said Ernest, calmly. "I see nothing—"

But Josefa had risen and stood before him with extended arms.

"He was my husband," she said, simply.

"We can now be happy, sweet love. Are you not satisfied to have waited?"

A kiss was his answer.

———

On Conti street, not far from the Mortgage Office, this little sign can be seen:

MORRISON & FATAH,
LAW AND NOTARIAL OFFICES.

The junior partner is a grandson of Ernest Fatah, the Creole poet and author.

———

THE END.

THE
STRANGLER OF CONGO SQUARE.

10

THE STRANGLER OF CONGO SQUARE.

I.—THE MANUSCRIPT.

One morning in the latter part of April, 1887, I was busily ticking away at my *Caligraph*, when a cheery voice startled me with this remark:

"Hello, old man!"

I looked up and perceived Yates Stinton, my college chum and inseparable companion.

"Well, what's up?" I ventured, grasping his extended hand. "Don't stay an eternity in expressing yourself, I entreat you; am tremendously busy to-day."

"All right, I waive prefatory remarks: Published any stories lately?"

"Not a line since November last; too much office work."

"Feel like launching a stunner?"

"If I can get good stuff, yes."

"I can furnish you all the material needed, having unearthed the strangest manuscript ever brought to light. Come over this evening and I'll show it to you.''

'' Anything else?''

I nervously toyed with the keys of my type-writer.

"You are deliciously polite this morning," observed Stinton, giving me a parting shake. "You will surely be around, eh?''

"Yes. So long.''

"Crick! Crick!" went the cylinder, as I fed in a new sheet and resumed work in earnest.

Seven was striking when I entered Stinton's room that evening, with this query on my lips:

"Well, where's that unparalleled phenomenon?''

"I'll get it in a minute," was the answer.

He opened a drawer of his book-case and brought out a roll of paper, which he handed me, saying:

"Just go over those pages and tell me how you like the narrator's style. It is just the sort of nonsense you always write about—intensely romantic love.''

I was soon deeply interested in the document. For fully two hours I read on, Stinton in the meantime smoking and pretending to read, but

I could see he was watching the expression of my face. I finally laid down the manuscript and said:

"This can make a capital romance, Yates. I'll take care of it."

"Do you not think it too immoral?"

"As it now reads, decidedly."

"You will then edit it?,'

"Yes, but I will have to wait until Court adjourns *sine die*. As you know, there's nothing of much importance to do about the clerk's office from June until November and I can then devote all my time to it."

I again scrutinized the manuscript and observed:

"I say, old fellow, where did you resurrect this? Judging from its mustiness, I have no hesitancy to believe it was brought over from the Old Country by DeSoto."

"Found it in an old book store on Exchange Alley the other day," observed Stinton, nervously drumming with his fingers on the table and averting my gaze. "Paid a quarter for it, a bargain which seemed to raise a suspicion in the book-seller's mind that I was a crank. He had thrown it away as rubbish, and as his shop

is luckily never swept out, escaped destruction.
I read the story, thought it weird and interesting and reasoned you could weave something
out of it.''

"Do you know anything about its history?''

"Not a syllable.''

"Well, let it rest. I'll have all summer to
work this up. What do you say to a game of
chess? You annihilated me last Sunday and I
thirst for revenge.''

We were soon deeply engrossed in our favorite pastime, and it was long after midnight before we gave the chessmen a rest.

About a week after my visit to Stinton's, he
left New Orleans for Paris, France, whither he
went with the intention of perfecting his studies.
It seems to me I still see him waving a regretful
farewell from the deck of the *Ville de Paris* as
she steamed into midstream. Poor fellow, I
wonder if he ever reached his destination? Although he had promised to keep me faithfully
posted about his whereabouts, I have never
heard from him.

On the third day of July, 1887—as is the
yearly custom in New Orleans—the principal
courts adjourned until November following.

There being very little stenographic or type-writing work to do, I found myself at leisure to investigate the history of Stinton's manuscript and discovered that he had told me a stupendous fib. The crusty book-seller in Exchange Alley expressed unfeigned surprise when I broached the subject and could not recollect having ever seen a person answering Stinton's description. This, coupled with the latter's unexplained silence, renders the matter still more bewildering, and I have been wondering to this day what could be his motive in concocting such a fable and entrusting me with this strange old record. I have of late made a remarkable discovery, which, instead of clearing away the mysterious haze which surrounds this manuscript, renders the matter still more aggravating—Stinton's grandmother was named Edna Narbour. I will not attempt to theorize upon this coincidence. It will avail nothing, as the last descendant of the Narbours was Yates Stinton.

II.--CONGO SQUARE.

On Rampart street, between St. Peter and St. Ann, and about five minutes' walk from

Canal street, is Congo Square. It is one of the prettiest parks in New Orleans, having an elegant circular fountain in the center and inviting shade trees scattered here and there. It is the favorite resort of children and their nurses, and presents an animated, interesting sight every evening—for the weather is never continuously cold enough in New Orleans to prevent out-door exercise.

Years ago Congo Square was nearly a waste, its tall, rank grass affording convenient hiding places for a dangerous, unruly element which prowled about at night and rendered the locality unsafe for belated pedestrians on Rampart and adjoining streets. The footpads became so bold and their robberies so frequent, that the residents of the Second District organized themselves into a mutual protective association and subscriptions were raised to reclaim and beautify the park. The weeds were cut, trees trimmed, shelled walks laid out and lamp-posts erected where they would do the most good. The thugs and sand-baggers abandoned the locality and reopened business in the neighorhood of the Old Basin, where their depredations are still narrated with whispered awe.

Not long after the inauguration of these improvements, excavations were begun in the center of the square for the building of the present fountain. One day a workman was seen to suddenly disappear with a yell of terror, the piled-up earth falling after him. As soon as they had recovered from their surprise, his companions went to his rescue, working cautiously and apprehensively, and soon came upon his insensible body. He was brought back to the open air, restoratives were applied and he soon regained his senses, proving to have been only badly frightened, but not hurt in the least. In the meantime, his fellow workmen had been investigating the cause of the trouble. They came upon a small tunnel, which, upon being cleared of the debris which choked it, widened into a cave about 20 by 30 feet in diameter. In the center was found a heap of bones, presumably a human skeleton. Commenting upon the occurrence, the old *New Orleans Chronicle* editorially says:

"About a year before the breaking out of the Mexican War, this city was terrorized by a series of mysterious murders near Congo Square. The victims were invariably women, who were in every instance strangled to death. The police were kept on the alert from sunset to sunrise, but the fiend was never captured. Several times he was chased and closely pressed, but he seemed to vanish into the air as soon as he entered the Square. The discovery of the cave explains the mystery."

From what could be ascertained from the musty records on file at the Central Police Station, this cave was used by the marauders who then infested the locality to hide their plunder. It had long ago been forgotten.

III.—THE STORY.

In the year 1845, a Spanish company established a large cigar manufactory in New Orleans, the first of its kind to operate upon an extensive scale in Louisiana. The general manager was one Miguel Zucci, a young man not yet thirty, handsome, conceited, and a boasted twirler of feminine hearts. Having flattering credentials, he was cordially welcomed into the exclusive social world of the Southern metropolis.

Alice Narbour, the belle of the *Quartier Creole* and a reputed flirt, resolved to humble the arrogant Castilian and make him sway to

her every whim and caprice. Her less worldly
sister, Edna, warned her to be careful in her
behavior towards the young man, as she was
afraid the revengeful spirit of his race would
prompt him to do her harm should he fall
seriously in love with her. But Alice only smiled
defiantly and continued to enslave the boastful
foreigner.

On a sultry, drizzling evening in June, 1845,
the sisters were seated near a window of their
fashionable Esplanade Avenue residence, gazing
ruefully at the pattering rain.

"I wonder if our gallant friend will brave
the elements?" observed Alice, tracing fantastic designs upon the hazy window pane with
her rosy finger. "I presume he will, Doolie.
I don't think a West Indian hurricane could
stop him."

She laughed and turned to her companion for
approval; but the latter reprovingly said:

"You should cure yourself of that horrible
mania of flirting, dear. No good can come of
it."

"Bah, you little moralist; there's no harm at
all. It is pure, simple fun. If men are foolish
enough to believe all the nonsense I whisper,
they are worthy to be duped."

"But you go too far. Look at Miguel's case, for instance. I am sure he loves you truly."

"Does he? I am indeed glad to hear it. He thinks too much of himself and I want to make him feel we are his superiors."

Edna shrugged her shoulders.

"Do as you wish," she said, "but I advise you to leave him alone!"

"I can't, Doolie," pouted Alice. "He is getting so interesting. I expect him to be at my knees before long."

Edna took Alice's hand in hers.

"Do not go that far, dear," she pleaded. "I have a presentiment that evil will happen."

"Tut, tut. You are a pessimist. It is true he is deplorably conceited, but Miguel is a gentleman after all and would not feel offended if he found out I was flirting him."

Edna sighed and observed:

"Keep on, then. But I do not feel at all at ease. Miguel comes of a hot-headed, imperious race, and I am sure he will allow no girl to make fun of him."

Alice was thoughtful a few moments.

"Do you think he would do anything terrible if I told him I was flirting?" she asked.

"I do," was the decided answer. "You have been too attentive to him."

"What can he do? Do you think he would kill me?"

"I do not say he will go that far, but he will get even some way or other. This life is too short to wilfully make enemies."

"Miguel my enemy? That would be grand, Doolie. It would be so delightfully romantic. I think I'll try the experiment by giving him his *congé* to-night."

Edna looked earnestly into her sister's face.

"Do not do that, Alice. You will regret it. I have noted the expression of his face when he speaks of you, and one can plainly see he loves you desperately."

Alice sat down on Edna's knees and passed her arms around her neck.

"You dear, silly, scolding pet, how do you know I do not love him?" she said, in altered tones.

Edna looked into the roguish eyes and dubiously said:

"If you do, I make full apologies. But it is

hard to believe. You are too volatile to think seriously of anything.''

'' But I *am* serious, Doolie. I only want to see what he will say and then I'll consent to be his wife. It looks so provincial to fly into a young man's arms as soon as he confesses his adoration.''

Edna glanced at the whimsical girl and said :

''Act according to your fancy, but be prudent. It is a risky thing to trifle with love.''

Alice's answer was a cordial hug, and she resumed her vigil by the window.

'' I wonder what can be keeping him away,'' she observed. '' He is intelligent, and ought to know that no other visitors would dare to come in such weather. It's nearly seven, too. Ah, here he is. Let him think I am alone, Doolie. Run up stairs, and I'll call you when the drama is over.''

'' Just as you wish, my dear,'' said Edna. '' But mind what I said.''

She warningly shook her finger and tripped up the carpeted staircase.

*   *   *   *   *   *   *

Half an hour later Edna came to the head of the stairs and peeped curiously below.

" How still they are down there," she solil-
oquized. " I wonder what they are doing?
The gas is not even lit. Miguel couldn't have
gone, for Alice would have joined me. Perhaps Alice spoke the truth and really loves him,
after all. He is a good match—a little self-
loving, it is true, but he is young yet. Girls are
so funny, anyhow. I'll just creep to the parlor,
and who knows if I will not find them hugging
each other? Won't they jump, though, when
I poke my head in!"

She tip-toed softly down and soon reached
the parlor. All was silent. She stretched her
head through the open door, but could not see
nor hear anything. Beginning to feel frightened, she said:

"Alice—Mr. Miguel—where are you? Joking
aside, I am afraid."

No reply.

" Oh dear, what can be the matter? Alice,
speak out. You know how nervous I am. Oh,
you rascals, I'm sure I'll find you on your
favorite sofa!"

She felt her way to the sofa. It was un-
occupied.

"If I only had a light," thought the now terrified girl.

She felt about for the mantelpiece and found the match-safe. She eagerly took out a match and scratched it against the wall. The phosphorus sputtered, flickered and went out. Not discouraged, the trembling girl lit another match and, as it finally brightly burned, looked searchingly about. As she did so, her eyes rested upon the insensible form of her sister. Her senses reeled, she gave a piercing scream and sank into unconsciousness.

IV.—MIGUEL ZUCCI'S CONFESSION.

The subjoined confession, addressed to "Senorita Edna Narbour," and written in Spanish, was found by the editor of this narrative in a drawer of Stinton's cabinet. A faithful translation is given:

NEW ORLEANS, July — , 1845.

MISS—You have always been so kind to me, I think it proper to bare my heart to you. Pause and think before censuring me. I loved with an intensity which bordered on insanity. I was deceived * * * The rest all the world knows.

The papers have been very clamorous about my actions lately. The strangling of that beautiful girl last Tuesday seems to have aroused them into a frenzy and the police have increased their vigilance. I fear to creep out of my den, for detection means the gallows. I prefer dying by my own hands.

I hope you will pardon the breach of etiquette I commit in using a pencil to write this. To-night I will steal out to mail you this communication, but I dare not stir by daylight to get writing materials. I am too weak with hunger and fever and will excite suspicion.

But I must hurry. My fingers feel stiff and cramped, my eyes burning and misty.

    *   *   *   *   *   *   *

Two weeks ago, while the skies were weeping and the elements turbulent, I sought the only woman on earth I devotedly loved. She met me at the door, a smile on her lips, and said:

" I was standing at the window and saw you coming, Mr. Miguel, and thought I might just as well save you further drenching."

" You are very kind," I replied, my heart

11

wildly beating with happiness; "I thought you would give me a lecture for calling in such weather."

" O no, far from it." was the cordial answer; " I world have felt so lonesome all alone in this dismal house. Doolie took dinner out and has not yet returned, you know."

We then entered the parlor. We conversed upon current topics, but our remarks gradually became personal. Alice's head being invitingly near, I captured a peeping curl and said :

"I wish I was the owner of this treasure."

Alice made no reply, but cast down her eyes. Encouraged, I resumed :

" I wish I could also possess something dearer, purer, more sublime—"

Alice's wondering look stopped me.

" What are you talking about, Mr. Zucci?" she said, with a rudeness which astounded me. " I hate rhetorical phrases. They remind me of oriental salutations."

" I will be plainer," I said, taking her hand in mine. " I love you."

"I know you do," answered the girl, withdrawing her hand.

" Then why do you elude me?"

"Because I do not care for you," was the cold response.

I smiled incredulously.

"You are jesting, Alice," I said.

"No, sir, I am not. I was having fun with you, that is all. I was told you hated women and wanted to see if the rumor was unfounded. I see you were courteous enough to make an exception in my case. I presume you will now say I am a flirt?"

"Far from it," I answered, a tremor in my tones. "If I fostered such a thought, I would cease to love and respect you. You are too good, too pure, to wound a trusting heart. I understand that a man can be hypocritical; but a woman—never. You love me, do you not?"

I passed my arm around her waist and drew her to me.

"I—I don't, Mr. Miguel," stammered the girl, frightened by my impetuous words. "Leave me go, sir. It is getting dark and I must light the gas."

"Light the gas? Of course not. This would spoil the romance of love making."

I tried to embrace her, but she struggled and ran away from me. Again I caught her and was about to kiss her taunting lips, when she angrily exclaimed:

" If you are a man of honor, stop instantly !"

I released my grasp and gazed with frowning features into the girl's face.

" Do you really mean this?" I said brokenly. " Is it possible that you have been toying with me ?"

Alice seemed stung by my peremptory tones and defiantly answered :

"Assuredly, sir. You are indeed presumptuous to think otherwise."

Without a word and before she could make a movement, I seized her by the throat. She tried to scream, but it was too late. Her eyes grew wild and strange, my clutch tightened, and my darling's fair form fell senseless to the floor. It was only then that I saw the enormity of my crime. But I did not regret it. I had loved, she had nurtured my passion, deceived me,— I could not help it.

Pardon me, dear miss, if I repeat that I do not regret what I have done. Even now, as I stand on the brink of eternity and think of the tortures an immortal life may mete to my erring soul, I feel happy in the thought that I have slain this false girl. God or the devil, whatever be the ruling power where our souls will meet, grant that I may have full control of her spirit, that I may inflict upon it unceasing torments.

MIGUEL ZUCCI.

THE END.

IYALA, THE DANCER.

IYALA, THE DANCER

I.

"Tonk, tonk, tonk, tonk!"

The old clock in the banking house of Gizaille & Co. discordantly clanked the closing hour; but the sound seemed a melody to the tired clerks.

"Four o'clock, Lightning," observed Oswald Lepense, playfully tapping Edgar Socsy, the the general book-keeper, on the shoulder.

Edgar smiled good-humoredly, but there was a tinge of annoyance in his tones as he remarked:

"I can't explain it, but I'm all tangled up. And I wanted to get off early, too."

"Let me give you a lift," said Oswald. "I'm through for the day."

Edgar accepted. The young men worked assiduously and had everything in order when the half hour sounded.

The pair walked home together. The dis-

tance being short and the air brisk, they cared
not to ride.

"Are you going to the opera to-night?" ventured Oswald."

"No," replied Edgar. "I promised Paulette
to bring her to see *The Private Secretary* at
the Grand."

"You'll miss a fine treat."

"Anything extra?"

"The star is too hoarse to sing and little Iyala
will take the role of *Carmen*— Well, what's
the matter?"

For Edgar had nearly stopped in his walk and
seemed confused about something.

"Oh, nothing," was the calm reply; "your
cigar scorched my hand and it made me feel a
little creepy."

"I'll prevent further cremation by smoking
it," said Oswald.

He placed the weed to his lips. It was un-
lighted!

The young man looked searchingly at his
companion.

"You must have been dreaming," he remarked. "This cigar has been fireless for at least
ten minutes. There is even no smoke in it."

"I guess my hand put out the last spark," said Edgar, uneasily.

"Possibly," replied Oswald, incredulously. "If I had such sensitive hands, I'll keep them in my pocket. Well, here's my shanty. Sorry you can't be around to-night."

"I might drop in during the last act."

Oswald dubiously shook his head.

"Tut, tut," he said; "by the time you escort your betrothed home and bid her good night, everything will be dark around the old French."

"Anyhow, I'll try," responded Edgar.

A smile was on his lips, but it was a veil for his tumultuous heart.

II.

Oswald Lepense and Edgar Socsy were intimate friends. They had studied side by side at Spring Hill College—that historic Jesuit institution which has given so many brilliant lights to the world—and had both graduated with high honors. When they returned to their native city they had found employment in the same bank and were inseparable co-workers.

The season of French opera had just begun. Manager Lemaire had brought from Europe a delightful troupe, attached to which was a splendid *corps de ballet*. Mlle. Iyala, the *premiere danseuse*, had from her initial appearance captivated the undefended hearts of the youths and baldheads. Among her clandestine admirers was Edgar Socsy, who took care that his amours were carefully concealed from his fiancée. He loved Paulette sincerely and was certain he would make a kind and model husband, but he saw no harm in having fun with the vivacious little dancer. She would be in romantic Spain, flirting new admirers, long before his wedding day dawned.

Edgar found Paulette seated pensively near the fire when he entered. Her face beamed when she saw him.

"How late you are!" she said, helping him to divest himself of his heavy coat.

"A little more I would have stayed until 6 or 7."

"Another clerk sick? Something is always wrong with your old bank."

"No, it was my fault. I got my additions all mixed up. Fortunately, Oswald came to my assistance."

" How foolish of you! They say you are always so correct and punctual, too. What was the matter to-day?"

"I suppose I think too much of you," was the whispered answer, followed by a kiss.

She laughingly threatened him with her finger and they sat down for a little chat before dinner.

" By the by," observed Paulette, " did you buy tickets for the Grand already?"

" Yes; here they are."

The blue eyes had a disappointed look.

" I'm sorry you did. I saw by the papers that the French troupe would play *Carmen* to-night, and I am just dying to see it."

" But Mlle. Minetta is ill and will be replaced by the *premiere danseuse*."

" Can she act also? I thought she could only dance."

"Oswald told me she would play to-night."

Paulette was thoughtful a moment.

"I wish I could go," she said, longingly.

"It is not too late," remarked Edgar. "I can take a run to the box office immediately after dinner and get two parquets. If these are not obtainable, we can fall back on the *premieres* or *secondes*."

"And what will you do with the tickets for the Grand."

"Frame them."

The girl looked reprovingly at him.

"No, this would be foolish. We need all the spare cash we have to start house-keeping and it would not do to squander two dollars so recklessly. I'll see *Carmen* another time."

"Just as you wish, my Queenie," said Edgar. "So long as you are satisfied. I have nothing to say. Come, here's the dinner-bell."

She took his proffered arm and they sought the dining-room.

III.

The Private Secretary had been given to a crowded house.

" Do you regret your outburst of economy?" asked Edgar Socsy to his affianced, as they proceeded homeward.

" No, indeed," was the response. " I am delighted with the play."

An assertion which she proved by making it her entire theme until they reached home. The lovers then separated, Paulette seeking her room and Edgar going as far as his own, but silently stealing out a few moments afterward. He had to keep his word with Oswald.

Mlle. Iyala had scored an unparalleled success. Her acting was voted superb and the young bloods went wild over her.

" It is evident that her talents do not cling to her feet." whispered Oswald to a companion.

Edgar found only standing room, but managed to crowd to the front and was soon satisfied his ideal had noticed him. Yes, she even seemed to glance straight at him when she trilled her most passionate love songs, and he felt more bewitched than ever.

A private room in the *Café des Artistes* held a gay couple that night. For the first time, Iyala had consented to honor Edgar with her sole companionship, and ere the supper was over, had promised to reject other suitors and love only him.

For a few weeks the lovers were happy. But slighted rivals became jealous of Edgar's monopoly, and one morning an anonymous letter disclosed the state of affairs to Paulette. She flushed indignantly at such an insinuation and resolved at once to seek her betrothed and hear the truth from his own lips.   It was not yet ten, and she could never wait until evening with such a burden on her mind.

"A lady wishes to speak to Mr. Socsy," said the janitor.

Edgar stepped out and was not a little surprised to see his fiancée. With much self-control she requested a few moments' secret conversation. Edgar bade her enter the private office and she showed him the traitorous letter. The young man's face blanched as he read the missive.

"Is this true?" asked Paulette, falteringly.

He made no reply, but gazed stupidly at her.

"Answer!" she angrily said, grasping his arm.

"For heaven's sake, do not make a scene here, Paulette," pleaded Edgar, looking apprehensively at the door.

"Pride will not permit me to do so," was the calm reply. "You then admit you have been fooling me?"

"I—I did not do so to—"

"Answer yes or no."

"Yes."

"And you will see her again to-night?"

"She expects me."

Paulette looked her lover full in the face.

"If you do," she said, determinedly, "all is over between us. I forgive you so far because I love you, but if you even speak to that serpent again, you may obliterate me from your memory. That is all. Edgar. Do not let your face betray us."

They smilingly left the room, the envious clerks craning their necks to catch a glimpse of the lovely girl.

"Socsy is a lucky dog," said Oswald, in an audible whisper.

Edgar smiled feebly in acknowledgment and resumed his duties. But his co-workers remarked he was inexplicably ill at ease as the hours sped by.

IV.

"Tonk, tonk, tonk, tonk!"

Edgar roused himself from his reveries and gazed vacantly at his open book. His work was hardly half finished.

Oswald, whose chief aim in life was not to tarry at the bank as soon as the last stroke of

12

four had sounded, reached for his hat, preparatory to going home. Edgar beckoned to him.

" Well, what's the racket?" was the cheery remark.

Edgar pointed to the blank pages.

" What!" exclaimed his surprised friend. " You may just as well send home for your pillow, Slowcoach. I've been watching you, and I am decidedly glad she does not come here every day. Why, how pale you are!"

" I do not feel well, Os., and want you to balance for me. I had better go home and rest."

For answer, Oswald placed his hat on its accustomed peg.

" Clear out, then," he said pleasantly. " Not having any blue eyes and golden hair to render me idiotic, I'll post that book in a jiffy."

Edgar thankfully pressed his hand and departed. He did not go home, but sought Iyala and explained his predicament to her.

" We must part, Yola," he said, regretfully. " I did not want to cowardly abandon you. I can not break the poor orphan's heart. Not only would I feel miserable, but the whole world will blame me."

Iyala's eyes were aflame with anger.

"So you really love her?" she said.

Edgar looked up in genuine surprise.

"Of course, Yola."

"Why have you been telling me such lies, if you love another? You swore you were faithful to me."

"But a fiancée is a different thing, Yola," observed Edgar, frightened by her fervid passion. "She will be my wife."

"And I am only your toy?"

Her red lips curled contemptuously.

"Don't be absurd, Yola," observed Edgar.

"You surely did not expect that I would marry you."

"I do not care for a priest's blessing nor the stupidities of law. I love you and I intend to keep you."

"You must be reasonable, Yola. Think of the scandal which will burst out if you act unwisely. Old Gizaille is the cream of morality and will surely discharge me."

There was a baleful look on Iyala'a eyes and she was pensive a few moments. She presently observed:

"Do you remember the first night I played Carmen?"

Edgar nodded.

"Do you recall what prompted Don José to kill his sweetheart?"

"Yes."

The dark eyes sparkled dangerously.

"I always *did* approve him," was the calm observation.

Edgar laughed mockingly.

"The señoritas of Seville are ferocious, my dear." he said. "Adieu, tigress."

He bowed ceremoniously and departed. He met Oswald while walking down Bourbon street and told him everything in confidence.

"You had better be on your guard," was the parting caution. "I always heard that those dark-eyed girls were holy terrors."

Edgar shrugged his shoulders and proceeded homeward. Paulette welcomed him with customary tenderness. When they were alone, she sat nearer to him and said:

"Have you chosen?"

Edgar took the cold little hand in his.

"You are still my queen," he fondly said. "Forgive me."

A tear gemmed her lashes.

"You nearly broke my heart," was the gentle response; "I see you love me dearly, however, and make no reproaches."

They remained pensive for some time. Paulette finally observed :

"I hear that the second representation of *Carmen* takes place to-night. Will you escort me?"

Edgar's heart throbbed irregularly.

"I would be very happy to do so," he said, with forced cheerfulness, "but it is impossible to get seats. The box office was jammed when I passed Verlouin's music store this evening."

Paulette smilingly thrust her hand within her bosom and held forth a small envelope.

"I anticipated the rush and bought those since yesterday. Am I not a fine business woman?"

"Indeed you are," said Edgar, with feigned admiration.

Aye, the Fates were cruelly probing his wounded heart.

V.

Never before had the rôle of Carmen been played with such fervency. The bravi were

continuous and deafening. Iyala's sinuous
form swayed beautifully, her voice was loud
and clear, her aplomb inimitable.

Pale and restless, Edgar watched her every
movement. She had noticed him from the
first and had acted solely to enchain and be-
wilder him. He felt her glances penetrate to
the inmost recesses of his soul. Would she be
mad enough to carry out her threat? No, such
things only happened in novels.

The curtain fell on the last scene amid
tumultuous applause. The vast audience gaily
filed out, praising the fair young actress. Like
one in a dream, Edgar followed the crowd,
making monosyllabic replies to Paulette's chat-
ter. When they reached the foyer, he stopped
to help the girl arrange her wraps. Some one
touched him lightly on the shoulder. He turned
around and perceived Iyala, her eyes flaming,
her hand concealed within the folds of her cor-
sage.

" The senoritas of Seville honor their vows,"
she said, swiftly raising her arm. There was a
gleam, a startled cry from Paulette, and those
who looked back in affright saw Edgar Socsy
totter and fall.

" CLANG! CLANG! CLANG!"

The ambulance rushes through the deserted streets. As it dashes around corners and rumbles through the narrow thoroughfares, loudly sounding its warning, revelers returning from the French Opera House pause a moment in their laudations of Iyala to conjecture what unfortunate is in need of help; but before they have collected their bewildered thoughts, the wagon of mercy has disappeared in the darkness.

" CLANG! CLANG! CLANG, CLANG!"

Cars stop, carriages give precedence, people hurry out of the way.

" C-l-a-n-g!"

The crowd presses eagerly forward as the wagon stops. The students alight, run up the ancient stairway—

But it is too late.

———

THE END.

THE DEATH-ANGEL.

A LEGEND OF THE MIDDLE AGES.

THE DEATH-ANGEL.

A Legend of the Middle Ages.

The historical events which furnish the basis for this narrative happened centuries ago, when civilized Europe trembled with apprehension at the frequent impetuous inroads of oriental and occidental fanatics, whose inherent belief in predestination rendered them fearless of peril.

It was at that epoch that the Christian kings, becoming alarmed at the audacious invasion of the infidels, sanctioned the organization of the various military and religious orders which flourished in the Old World for nearly two hundred years. These societies worked contemporaneously with the crusades and were chiefly instrumental in preventing the standard of Mahomet from penetrating into Central Europe.

When the second crusade was organized, among those who joined Conrad III, Emperor of Germany, in his zealous pilgrimage to the

Holy Land, was Prince Inwelf, an officer of the Imperial Staff.

Inwelf followed his sovereign throughout his unfortunate campaign in Asia Minor. When the Christian army was eventually cut to pieces by the irrepressible adherents of Noureddin, the infidel leader, and forced to retreat, the young prince was made prisoner and sent to Damascus. His captors being aware of his rank, demanded a large ransom. This not being forthwith obtainable, the captive was sent under a strong escort to an inland town, Damascus being adjudged too insecure.

When about two days' journey from their destination, the escort was attacked by a nomadic band of desert pilferers and overpowered. Inwelf valiantly defended himself, but the odds against him were too powerful. He soon succumbed, pierced through the breast by a scimitar thrust.

After assuring themselves that those composing the escort were either all dead or mortally wounded, the brigands hurried away, carrying with them whatever booty they could appropriate.

As the hours glided by, Inwelf intently

watched the waning moon. As it gradually grew less discernable, a feeling of uncontrollable fear possessed him.

"O Moon!" he cried, almost deliriously, "you are the only friend whose face I will ever again see on earth. Do not abandon me in my last moments. Though your rays are feeble, they are a consolation, and I feel less lonesome when they linger over me. Do not leave me. I am afraid to be alone."

As he ceased speaking, it seemed to Inwelf that the Queen of Night shone brighter and friendlier; but the illusion was momentary, for its beams grew fainter and fainter as the minutes sped by.

"O Moon!" again implored the youth, "you who have so often borne me company in my rovings, why do you desert me to-night? If you can not stay, send one of your beams to keep me company, that I may die in your embrace."

No sooner were these words uttered, than the desert was illumined by a soft, glowing light, as if some intensely iridescent object were near. Smiling gratefully at the moon, Inwelf closed his eyes. He heard a gentle noise and looked wonderingly about. A feminine form approached. Inwelf saw it was a being of exquisite grace and loveliness and his whole soul was thrilled with ardent love. He made an effort to arise, but sank back exhausted.

"You have called for a moon-beam to bear you company," began the apparition, in a voice of delicate sweetness and fervency; "I have heard your appeals and have come to silence them. Why are you so timorous to-night, you who so often fought with undaunted valor? Why afraid of the darkness, you who have many times gallantly warred, with not even the friendly moon-beam to direct your movements? Noticing how rapidly your courage was forsaking you—seeing how childish you were growing, I have come to relieve you of all terrestrial cares, and speed your soul into the Happy Land."

As Inwelf heard those words, his fear and astonishment were displaced by a feeling of undefined adoration. Eagerly extending his arms, he exclaimed:

"Who are you, most beauteous Seraph, from whose lips such celestial wisdom flows? You have no doubt eluded the vigilance of the guardians of Paradise, for no mortal has such eloquent thoughts. Now that you are near, death has no terrors for me. Oh, how sweet, how delightful to die, if one could spend his eternal life beside you! You divine well that death claims me and have no doubt come to lead me into the Invisible Land. Slay me, sweet one! Though I know not who you are, I gladly sway to your will.''

"Ignorant youth, to speak thus," was the gentle reproof, in tones of argentine cadence. "Have you not heard of the wanderings of Nisrilu, emissary of the Death-Deity? Know you not that I am timed to visit the earth; that my mission is to ease anguish? By simply touching a mortal, I release his soul from its case of clay and his body becomes indifferent to the corrosive influence of mundane elements —unless a mortal profanes it by his touch, when it crumbles into dust. I have sent more souls into Paradise than there are stars in the firmament. Your death will not be violent, for you will be ushered into the realms of immortality with your features as undisturbed as those of a sleeping child.''

Nisrilu approached Inwelf. Her hand was
nearly on his brow, when he shrank back and
piteously cried :

"Before you still my frame, most adorable
Nisrilu, tell me whence you come—speak of
your past existence. My wound no longer
troubles me; your presence has proved its
nepenthe."

"So long as I am nigh," replied Nisrilu,
staying her hand, "you shall experience no
suffering. The indelicacy of your query places
you in imminent peril and my indignation
prompts me to leave you to your fate; but you
are so young, so forlorn, that I will satisfy your
pardonable curiosity. You are the first mortal
who has pried into my past life without being
punished. * * * Listen: More than three
thousand moons ago, during the caliphate of
Haroun-al-Rashid, of the dynasty of the Abas-
sidos, there dwelt near Mecca a venerable
chieftain named Hiafar. He had for his companion a young daughter known as Nisrilu,
reputed to be a rare type of Arabian loveliness.
Haroun heard of Nisrilu's charms and com-
manded Hiafar to send her to his harem. The
father indignantly refused. Enraged by what

he considered an affront, the caliph sent a large
body of men to carry off the child and con-
fiscate the father's possessions. Hiafar re-
sisted and was put to death. As for Nisrilu,
she never could be found. It is recorded on
the tablets of Arabian legendary lore that the
Houris, taking pity on the persecuted girl,
transported her to Paradise and made her immortal. Tradition also says that when the
moon is in its last quarter, Nisrilu is allowed to
revisit her native land. She seeks the battle
fields of her race, her mission being to assuage
the torments of the wounded. Although you
are a giaour, your features please me and I will
now lead you into our glorious land. You have
caused me to tarry so long, that you are the
only one I can solace to-night. Look, the
moon's last beam is dying!"

Nisrilu placed her hand on Inwelf's brow
and softly caressed him. The youth attempted
to resist the somnolent sensation which overmastered him and made an effort to speak. His
lips trembled, parted—but no sound issued.
Wearily closing his eyes, he felt an irresistible
languor and sank into unconsciousness.

    *   *   *   *   *

Forty years elapsed between the second and

13

third crusades. During that interval, the infidels had ravaged Palestine and made the king
of Jerusalem prisoner. This and other out-
rages finally aroused the avenging spirit of the
Christians and another crusade was organized,
led by the emperor of Germany and the kings
of France and England.

After many reverses and a few successes, a
truce was concluded between the hostile forces,
the Christian army gaining the advantage.

On their return from Palestine, while cross-
ing a particularly arid plain, the remnant of
England's brave soldiery, led by Richard
Cœur-de-Lion, perceived an oasis in the distance and eagerly hurried toward it. When
the king came upon the stragglers, he saw
them grouped wonderingly about an object on
the ground. Answering his inquiring look, one
of his suite observed:

" Here sleeps a handsome knight, your high-
ness. He looks so happy, so tranquil, that we
wonder why the desert blasts were so lenient
to him. I fain will awake him, for those
ghoulish infidels will slay him after we are
gone."

The courtier stooped and laid his hand on

the youth's shoulder to arouse him—but he merely grasped a handful of ashes.

* * * * *

Even to this day, as the weary traveler plods his way through the vast solitudes of the East and the penetrating dust-clouds beset him, the natives reverently remark :

" These are the ashes of the happy dead ; the work of our beautiful Death-Angel!"

THE END

SELECTIONS FROM

"SMILES AND TEARS,"

NOW IN COURSE OF PREPARATION.

PARDONABLE CURIOSITY.

They were lovers, though the secret
   Never wholly had been told,
For she was a roguish maiden
   And reproved his passion bold.
" Mother will feel too distressful
   If you carry me away,"
Pouted she — and no persuasion
   Could that resolution sway.

One day he sought consolation
   In wild roamings through the wood,
And soon came upon a streamlet
   Where the landscape mirrored stood.
Long he gazed into the waters,
   Laughing, rippling at his feet,
Thinking of his truant sweetheart,
   Without whom life was effete.

Soon he saw the cherished outlines
   Of a face delightful, dear,
Slowly forming, archly smiling,
   In the tranquil waters clear.

"'T is a vision," fondly mused he.
  "Of a face I'll ever seek,
And my wounded heart seems solaced"—
  But he stopped, for on his cheek

He felt the sensation thrilling
  Of a breath like Heaven's wind,
And a voice with gladness faltered
  As an arm his neck entwined:
"Girls are curious"—and the bright eyes
  Sought again the singing brook—
"And I peeped just to discover
  How your future wife will look!"

THE ANGRY PESSIMIST.

Heed not what those red lips smiling
  Murmur lowly unto you,
Nor the look of love enthralling
  Beaming in those eyes so blue.
Take care that those hands caressing
  Fetter not your heart now free;
Push away those arms entrancing
  Held forth with such childish glee.

Love has but a brief existence
  In that bosom young and fair—
Has not e'en the frail consistence
  Of the evanescent air.
Shun that dulcet voice melodious,
  Toy not with that straggling curl—
Naught on earth is so perfidious
  As this ever-pleasant girl.

False the tears which gem her lashes,
  False her pensive, downcast eyes;
And her simulated blushes
  Glow on cheeks where candor dies.
Obey not those rich lips sentient
  Pouting for a lover's kiss—
Ere the sun adorns the Orient
  They will prove to you remiss.

MY SWEET LULETTE.

Since from her side she bid me go,
      My sweet Lulette,
My cheeks have lost their blissful glow,
      Sered by regret;

Her pouting lips my thoughts beguile,
　　Make me upstart,
And day and night her cruel smile
　　Appalls my heart.

I know this face which makes me start
　　I should accurse;
For memories dear to my heart
　　Hate I should nurse;
I know the blush which tints her cheek
　　Is falsehood's seal,
But when dark eyes pardon seek,
　　My senses reel.

When evening's glare swift disappears
　　Mid shades of night;
When glorious Luna coyly peers
　　And charms the sight;
When Philomel trills loud and clear
　　In yonder glade.
I feel that nothing is so dear
　　As this false maid.

This life is such a weary span,
　　Why should we grieve,
And wait till cheeks are withered, wan
　　Ere we forgive?

Though I well know she's wayward, flirt,
　　My sweet Lulette,
Her witchery my soul's deep hurt
　　Makes me forget.

THE GIRL-SUICIDE.

The tear-wet eyes no pain disclose,
　　The blood-stained breast is freed from sighs,
The anguished soul has sought repose
　　Within the realms of paradise.

She loved, she sinned—and mercy craved
　　From marble hearts who spurned her plea;
Despairing, lost, adjudged depraved,
　　Grim Charon's arms she grasped with glee.

The father kneeling by his child,
　　A frenzied feeling in his breast,
With cruel curses once reviled
　　Her trembling form with woe oppressed.

The throngs that scan her girlish face
　　And deck her bier with roses sweet,
In life had naught but thorns to place
　　Beneath her wearied, erring feet.

Pride in this world so soon is crushed,
  Life so replete with grief and fears,
Why wait till hearts their throbs have hushed
  To shed regretful, useless tears?

Thus has it been for cycles past.
  So will it be till mankind dies—
We seek to ease the lives we blast
  When taunting Death all arts defies.

ESTRANGED.

Peace?   The word can ne'er be told,
For the slighted heart is cold:
Naught but everlasting hate
In my bosom you create.

Love?   Your cruel wiles have slain it
And your falsity entombed it:
Let its grave remain unsullied.
Let its ashes mould unpitied.

Go—I see your purpose fell:
Pardon would you have me tell?
I'd see you writhe in Hades' flame
Ere from your hand I mercy claim.

BABY.

[*To Master Adolph DeBlanc.*]

Hush! Speak low and softly, step with muffled
    tread—
Baby is reposing in its cozy bed.
He is such a rover, plays and screams so
    much.
That, poor thing, he's tired—No, not e'en a
    touch !
When his eyes he opens you may kisses
    take :
Do not now caress him, lest he should awake.

You ought to have seen him when he came to
    me
And, his eyes half-closing, sought my arms
    with glee.
"How much do you love me, darling baby-
    boy ?"
Asked I, kissing, eating, those plump cheeks
    with joy.
Swift the little bare arms wide were spread
    apart
And the wee lips babbled : "Big like Papa's
    heart !"

He can count to twenty. names the months and
    years,
Gets his Papa's slippers when his step he
    hears.
He repeats his prayers without troublous aid—
But is oft in dreamland ere the end is said.
He is—O, the rascal, see his eyes so blue
Gazing at us, shining like the sparkling dew!

TIN-A-FEEX.

[The odd character depicted below is a familiar type in New Orleans.
His outfit consists of a small furnace, a few tools and some solder. His
business is to renovate tin utensils, his outlandish cry being a corrup-
tion of "Any tin to fix."]

The morning light was dawning fast,
As through the streets there slowly passed
A man, who clutched with grimy hand
A furnace, on which there was penned:
    " TIN-A-FEEX ! "

His eyes were dull, his clothes besplashed
His face looked like a berry smashed;
And like a Choctaw's war-cry rang
The accents of his deaf'ning twang:
    " TIN-A-FEEX ! "

Through half-oped gates his neck he craned
And his vocation loud explained,
In tones which made the house-girls wild,
And tired mankind's rest beguiled:
    " TIN-A-FEEX ! "

" Go pawn your voice," the newsboy said,
" And lose the ticket, shaggy head,
Ere with a mud ball you are sprawled."
But with a scowl the old man bawled:
    " TIN-A-FEEX ! "

" O, fiend!" the nervous man complained,
" I wish in Hades you were chained!"
A fierce light glowered in his eye—
But still uprose that ceaseless cry:
    " TIN-A-FEEX ! "

" Meander in this cozy place,
And with some rye your thirst displace."
Thus spake the saloon-keeper sly,
As nearer drew that startling cry:
    " TIN-A-FEEX ! "

   *   *   *   *   *   *   *

At dead of night, as clanging fast,
The patrol wagon rattled past,
From 'neath a crumbling kitchen stair
A voice roared through the tranquil air:
    " TIN-A-FEEX ! "

A maudlin man the guardians bold
Soon in their grasp did firmly hold;
Aloft he waved a furnace small,
On which was writ this mud-stained scrawl:
  " Tin-a-Feex ! "

Upon the wagon's hardened floor,
They rushed him to the prison door;
Then, as the turnkey locked him in,
He yelled forth with uproarious din:
  " Tin-a-Feex ! "

THE FLEETING IDEAL.

I.

As a thoughtful youth was strolling
  Up a scenic Alpine path,
Under dewy bowers lolling
  To escape the sunlight's wrath —
He came to a gurgling fountain,
  From which flowed a torrent deep,
Leaping swiftly down the mountain
  With a reverberant sweep.

As he gazed about, delighted,
   He descried a lovely girl
On the sparkling verdure seated,
   Toying with a straying curl.

She was graceful, tall and lissom,
   With eyes of the softest blue,
And her face, so frank and handsome,
   Mirrored what her pure heart knew.
'Neath her throat was clasped a myrtle,
   Symbol of love deep and true,
And a bridal rose did nestle
   In her hair of golden hue.
And the blood her face was mantling
   As her cherub lips confessed
To the youth the thoughts ennobling
   Nurtured in her virgin breast:

" I am Virtue.
               For long ages
   Have I waited, prayed for thee,
And on Time's eternal pages
   Have I traced thy name with glee.
When thou wert by God created,
   In my bosom Love was born,
And I knew I would be mated
   To thee one resplendent morn.
14

I will, sweet one, be as constant
  As the sun which gems the sky,
And I will my every moment
  Spend in bliss if thou art nigh.
Come, let those arms sweetly fold thee,
  Let those lips by man unpressed
Kiss away the cares that shroud thee
  And assuage thy soul distressed."

She stretched forth her white arms fondly,
  Calling him by names most dear—
But the stoic youth gazed coldly,
  Heeding not her fair lips near.
Pushing back the bare arms lovely
  Held forth with such witchery,
Smiling at her girlish folly,
  From her presence sauntered he.
And poor Virtue's eyes grew misty,
  Sunbeams shunned the sighing air:
But the Fates, scorning pity,
  Tolled the tocsin of despair.

II.

Soon the youth espied a grotto
  Gaily decked with flowers rare,
On which was inscribed this motto:
  "*Here dwells Love, the Debonair.*"

On a couch reclined a maiden,
  Young, voluptuous, sensuous, fair,
And with lips like roses laden
  With a ruby's lurid glare.
Smiling, she bade him draw nearer,
  Smoothed a place for him to rest,
Plucking leaf by leaf a larkspur
  Which her restless fingers pressed.

"Of thy life I was a portion,"
  Murmured she in accents low,
"Loving thee with wild emotion,
  In the shadowed long ago.
While thou wert my ardent lover
  And with joy my being thrilled,
I thought that my faith would waver
  Only when my heart was stilled.
But my mood was gay and changeful,
  And another's arms I sought,
Giving thee, so proud, disdainful,
  Not a solitary thought.
Aye, forgive! Entwine your darling
  As in days when bliss supreme
Sceptred us with sway enthralling
  And made life a radiant dream!"

Her voice with deep passion trembled
  As those burning words she said,

And, with fervency dissembled,
　　Drew his lips to hers so red.
But the unmoved youth repelled her,
　　Would not e'en glance allow,
And with harsh reproaches left her,
　　Striding off with furrowed brow.
With a sob the fickle maiden
　　Watched her lover fade from sight;
But ere stars on high did glisten,
　　Others made her sorrow light.

III.

Evening's glare was slowly mingling
　　With the shades of nascent night
As the youth came to a dwelling　　ı
　　In an arbor hid from sight.
Muffled strains of music thrilling
　　Charmed his soul, erst passive, drear.
And he heard a sweet voice trilling
　　Sonnets fond in accents clear.
As he stood and raptly listened
　　To that soft, melodious voice.
His eyes with emotion glistened
　　And he felt his heart rejoice.

With his senses madly whirling
　　And a palpitating heart,

Entered he the wondrous dwelling,
  Conquered by the chanter's art.
Seated where the sunlight waning
  Sent a pallid, fading beam,
Was a girl with dark eyes shining
  Like the diamond's dazzling gleam.
At the stranger archly smiling,
  For a moment waited she;
Then her guitar idly fondling,
  Weirdly sang this strain with glee:

"I am Pride.
          A kind thought never
  Found a haven in my breast,.
And I slay with joy each lover
  Whom my beauty hath distressed.
Tremble, youth, while sweet I warble
  And with melody enchain
Heart of thine erst cold as marble,
  Vaunted proof 'gainst worldly pain.
In my eyes the starlight's lustre
  Finds a dangerous retreat—
See, one glance thy heart doth shatter,
  Brings thee, pleading, at my feet.
Nay, I never will accord thee
  Even momentary joy:
Foolish youth, I look upon thee
  Merely as a pleasing toy!"

Eyes aflame with baleful anger,
　　Shining, star-like, through the gloom.
With a taunting peal of laughter,
　　Fled she from the scented room.
Gazed the youth with heart swift-beating,
　　As one thralled with sorcery;
Then, with eager cry upstarting,
　　In wild pursuit darted he.

L'ENVOY.

Though this transient world may mould.
　　As the countless ages roll,
What one seeks from man to hold
　　Will he struggle to control.

THE END.